The Baie-C

AND OTH...

RD

The Baie-Comeau Angel

AND OTHER STORIES

Wilfred Watson

NeWest

First Edition

Canadian Cataloguing in Publication Data

Watson, Wilfred, 1911–
  The Baie-Comeau angel and other stories

  ISBN 0–920897–29–0
  I. Title.
  PS8545.A885B3 1993   C813'.54   C93–091177–6
  PR9199.3.W37B3 1993

Cover design: Jingfen Zhang
Interior design: John Luckhurst/GDL
Editor for the Press: Shirley Neuman
Financial assistance: NeWest Press gratefully acknowledges the financial assistance of The Alberta Foundation for the Arts, The Canada Council, and The NeWest Institute for Western Canadian Studies.

Printed and bound in Canada by Hignell Printing Limited

NeWest Publishers Limited
Suite 310, 10359 - 82 Avenue
Edmonton, Alberta
T6E 1Z9

Contents

The Lice

1

There was a certain bishop of Edmonton who greatly deplored the behaviour of his congregation and of the people of Edmonton, whom he thought guilty of covetousness and greed, envy, sloth, drunkenness, gluttony and lechery, anger, vanity and pride. He would often talk about this matter with his two priests, especially with the younger, whom he loved. But they preferred to think of their congregation as being materialistic. No, no — said the bishop. He liked to call materialism, he said, by its older names. He would roll off on his tongue the Latin terms for the seven deadly sins: *superbia, invidia, iracundia, accidia,* etc. etc. When the people of Edmonton's actions deserved these labels, he wouldn't neglect to apply them, he told his subordinates. That is what these labels were for.

He preached a good many powerful sermons on the subject of the deadly sins. One Lent he preached a series beginning, Pride, and going on through the list of sins till he got to the last. His congregation took these tongue-lashings in a tolerant way. They — the serious people among them — agreed with their bishop about the nature of sin; but though they felt he was right to preach about the utter holiness of God and the deplorable filthiness of sin, they felt that the bishop didn't rightly understand the tenacious nature of sinfulness. How could he? He was a saintly-minded man, and had mastered his passions and appetites. It was easy for him to resist temptation — and besides, he was a priest, and not only that, getting on in years. He couldn't comprehend how difficult it is for the non-clergy, even when they had a mind to, to cure the sinfulness of Adam in our natures — especially with this demon of materialism attacking us from the radios and television sets, from the newspapers and the motion-picture houses, from magazines, advertising mail and shop-windows.

Mr. Dobbs, a good Christian, though heretical on the difficult topic of birth-control, said as much to the bishop one day. If only, he ended up by exclaiming, the people of this diocese could be made to *see* their sins — in all their ugliness — as you have described it — then, perhaps, father, then perhaps . . .

The bishop thought deeply about what Mr. Dobbs had said to him . . .

But no way to show his flock the nature of sin came to his mind . . .

If only sin *could* be made visible.

If only . . .

At length, he decided to take his difficulty to God.

If only, he said in his heart, God would make the sin of each sinner in the diocese into a hunchback, why, how many souls would be saved for the New Jerusalem, saved in fact from terrible damnation. If only . . . He shivered a little at the thought. Suppose his own hump were uglier and fatter and more conspicuous than the lump of sin on the backs of his flock? Suppose he himself were, in spiritual pride, uglier and fouler than any of his congregation? It would be for the good of his own soul, he decided, if any condition of sin in him were made manifest.

So the bishop worded an outright prayer, as the spiritual leader of his flock, to God, that the sins of his congregation and of himself, should be made visible to himself and to all of them.

Then he fell asleep.

The next morning was Sunday. It was, the bishop saw when he awoke from dreamless sleep, a glorious clear fresh sunny morning. The sun sang in the sky like an angel. The blue sky sang. The trees seemed to be wearing a fresher green than usual, as if they had been washed with rain during the night — perhaps they had — but no — the ground was dry. It was the sun shining through the marvellously clear air of Edmonton that made everything so clean and bright.

In church, when the bishop turned round to look over the new clothes and the clear faces of his congregation, the people themselves seemed newer and brighter and more colourful than ever before. The gay hats of the young girls . . . the red dresses . . . the shirts and trousers and jackets of the men . . . even the blacks of those who had come decently garbed in black . . . seemed to glow with the colour of the morning and of the sun outside.

A sombre thought struck the bishop. Perhaps there had been another of these false "sales" at the Westmount shopping centre . . . and this new look . . . this freshness was simply just that. It was then that the bishop remembered his thoughts about hunchbacks and his prayer to God the night before.

He glanced at the shoulders of his flock to see if his prayer had been — but no, and he said a 'Thy will be done' to himself, rather hastily. A terrible fear struck him. He wriggled his shoulders. They seemed, as he did so, rather odd. He squeezed his elbows to his side, trying to feel his back. He looked round, and finally, put his hand to his shoulder, as if — and this, he realized glumly was a deceit, a hypocrisy — he were adjusting his clothing. But no . . . his terrible prayer . . . God in his mercy . . . who sees all issues . . . had . . . in his wisdom . . . seen fit not to grant. *Non sum dignus* . . .

Introibo ad Altare Dei — *Adjutorium nostrum in nomine Domini* — I will go into the altar of God — Our help is in the name of the Lord . . . the bishop had got so far in the saying of the order of mass. And the confession was over, *Confiteor Deo omnipotenti, beatae Mariae semper Virgini* . . . I confess to almighty God, to blessed Mary ever a virgin . . . . The bishop had got as far as the absolution: *Misereatur vestri omnipotens Deus, et, dimissis peccatis vestris* . . . May almighty God have mercy upon you, and forgive you your sins.

It was then that the bishop's eyes fell upon the crucifix on the altar, for at this point he had to turn to the altar and say, silently,

Take away from us our iniquities, we beseech thee . . .

The words turned to ice in his throat.

For, streaming from the crucifix . . . was . . . terrible thing to see, a swarm . . . yes, swarm of some sort of insects . . . No, not streaming from it . . . but drawn to it . . . as if to a magnet . . . which was sucking them in . . . insects . . .

The bishop didn't know what to think. He wasn't sure what he ought to do . . . He prostrated himself, burying himself for a time in prayer . . .

Then he stood up before the crucifix . . . and yes . . . it was insects that were hanging in clusters there . . . as if a swarm of bees had alighted . . . as if the blessed crucifix were their queen . . . but, *domine misere*, it was not bees, but some small loathsome insects . . .

Lice . . . said the bishop. *Lice* . . . And then, in an instant the meaning of the miracle — for it was a miracle that his eyes were glazed by — dawned on him, as clearly as if an angel had told him. God had chosen his own way to make the sins of his congregation (and perhaps the sins of the people of Edmonton, too) visible to the eye of sense; he had chosen to turn these foul loathsome wickednesses, evil thoughts, covetousnesses, cupidities of the flesh, into lice polluting the crucifix.

Even when this realization had punctured its way into his mind, the bishop, like someone who has received a telegram of great importance, understands it, but remains unbelieving, put (or rather pushed) forward his arm, and stretched his finger out to touch one of the hideous things. . . . The insect was crushed by the doubting Thomas finger, and a drop of blood smeared — polluted the altar-cloth. Polluted? Ought he, the bishop fearfully checked himself, to conclude, *polluted*? Might not this blood be the blessed blood of the Redeemer of mankind? He sank feebly down upon his knees again, and hid himself in a state between trance and wordless prayer.

Not knowing what they should do, his priests and his acolytes, who had seen almost in the same instant (but with far less comprehension) what he had seen, came towards him, fearing that he had been overcome. But he pulled himself together, and signalled to them to turn to their ritual places.

And he went on, as if instructed by God Himself, in this emergency, with mass. He didn't realize what he was saying. In his mind two ideas were in conflict — swinging backwards and forwards like an irresistible pendulum, which swayed him with its motion. He thought: a miracle, a miracle. But his next thought was:

these sins have been turned into *lice*. As far as the glory of the one thought raised him up, the shame of the other sucked him down.

There were hanging to the crucifix, it seemed to him, all sorts of small noxious pestiferous blood-sucking insects. There was the common louse. There were bed-bugs, flat and stupid-looking discs of redness; and every sort of louse. He had seen — once, on the farm he was brought up on, a chicken-house hanging with ropes of chicken fleas; and he thought of the pecked rumps of these sorry infected fowl — their featherless backs bleeding where other chickens with no less melancholy backs, had beaked them, pecking at lice, but beaking through the skin. But no sight as horrible as the one before his eyes.

When the *credo* was over, he went down to the communion rail, and stood facing his flock. Casting his eye over them, as a shepherd counts his sheep, or as a father casts his eye over his children, he marvelled at their shining faces, at their shining clothes, at their shining presence — the light seemed to come from within them — they seemed like a churchful of angels, not people. The other swing of the pendulum compelled him. He didn't know what to say to them. It certainly wasn't a time for preaching. At last the words came, almost of their own.

"My children, turn round your heads and look at one another."

Surprised, they didn't at once obey him, but stared straight and fixedly at him.

"My children, look at one another."

Shyly, first one and then another turned round to look at his neighbour, and then, catching his neighbour's eye, turned back in a puzzled fashion to the old priest. It seemed to them he stood there in front of them like a shining angel.

"My children," he said over again, with smiling patience, "look at yourselves — turn round and look at yourselves. Take a good look at yourselves. It is a *good* look, isn't it?"

Less shyly this time, they did as they were told, and then turned their eyes back to the priest.

"What is it," he asked them, in the softest voice — in a voice not louder than a whisper — "what is it you see — what do you see? — You see," he told them, "the beauty of holiness adorning each one of you."

He stood silent for a long time.

At length he found words to tell them what had happened. "God has performed a wonderful miracle. We think in our hearts that there aren't any more miracles performed in this twentieth century after Christ's birth — we think God has lost the ability to do a miracle. But behold, God has performed one. God has shown each of you the beauty of human beings, even in this shape we stand in — it is a beautiful shape, if it isn't made ugly by sin."

He paused. "Look round you at yourselves again." They still didn't understand him, but they looked around about them, as he told them to.

"And now," he said to them, in a voice sepulchral and low — the voice of one buried in the grave, "look at the crucifix on the altar . . ."

Look at the crucifix on the altar . . . when he said this low-voiced injunction a second time, all their eyes were trained on the crucifix.

None of them could see clearly what it was that had darkened, had clouded over, the shining silver of the cross . . . and the bishop explained to them what had happened. As he spoke, the vision of brightness which he saw resting upon them, vanished.

In thrilling fatherly voice he implored them to gaze on the miracle, and see how God had made visible their sins to them, in the form of lice . . . *lice* which he had caused to infest the crucifix, nasty, loathsome, bloodsucking creatures, lice . . . fleas . . . and *bedbugs* . . . and this was why . . .

His voice trailed away into inaudibility, mere imploration. But everyone in the church understood what he was trying, and unable, to say.

2

When the news of the miracle spread to the world outside — as it very quickly did spread, a nine-day's wonder resulted.

The Edmonton *Journal* gave the miracle front-page headlines, and for several weeks reported daily on the ebb and flow of the swarm of insects to be seen clinging to the cross of the church. *Time* wrote up the miracle in a leading article, honoured the bishop with a cover portrait, and commented on the remarkable reticence he displayed — indeed, complained of it. In truth, he wasn't interested in this sort of fame. *Life* sent photographers to him, but the bishop refused them admittance to the church. Whether they did take photographs surreptitiously, or whether they manufactured them, photographs of the miraculously infested crucifix appeared, in the current issue of *Life*.

Even as far away as Rome, notice was taken of the "miracle of Edmonton," as it was soon called. The Vatican was bound to take an interest in it, for, as may be expected, scientists of a sceptical turn of mind asked to be allowed to test the validity of the alleged miraculous happening. The bishop, however, refused to allow them access to it. They challenged him in the name of truth. There was no lack of witness to the truth, he said. Many eyewitnesses of unimpeachable veracity testified to what had happened — and all that sceptics wanted to do was to find some way of throwing doubt on the occurrence.

The editor of the Edmonton *Journal* held the bishop's stand to be right. An editorial appeared which took the bishop's part against the scientists — this editorial pointed out that the saintliness of the bishop had done more for Edmonton in the way of publicity than anything else in the city's history, with the possible exception of the victories of the town's football team, the Eskimos. To this editorial, a University of Alberta classics professor replied caustically, in a letter, that he, for one, didn't want Edmonton to become another home of superstition, like Lourdes, in France.

As for the bishop, he withdrew his skirts with remarkable dexterity from all these unsavoury arguments about what had happened.

His heart indeed was set elsewhere.

And the next Sunday after the appearance of the lice, he rejoiced to notice that the swarm on the crucifix had very noticeably diminished. He might have attributed this lessening (or so I am inclined to think) to a waning of the force of the miracle. But he believed, as a result of their sins being made visible to them, his congregation had been at some pains to resist the temptations of sin; and that the crucifix was a gauge of their success.

When he spoke to them in church, that was what he said. "My children, I rejoice to see that . . ."

In a low voice, he begged them to try with all their hearts to continue the improvement of the past week . . . he knew that a long-settled-in habit of vice couldn't be cured in a few days . . . but God was helping them . . . and he said he looked forward to the time when the crucifix would be completely free of lice which still clung to it in swarms . . .

It is difficult, however, for human beings to resist temptation for periods of longer than a few days, even when all the world has its eye on what is happening; and the second Sunday after the miracle occurred showed a marked increase in the swarming lice.

The bishop in a reproachful voice recalled to his flock what was happening. They looked at his reproachful figure sadly, as if they were all signifying to him, we can't help it, but . . . we are flesh and blood, merely. They received what he said to them in patience, at least. It was not so on the *third* Sunday after the miracle. To the bishop, with anxious eyes on the crucifix of the church as a true gauge of the sinfulness of his people, it seemed, on this third Sunday after God had spoken to them with the plague of lice, as if his flock was more sinful than ever they had been.

His voice, though he tried to modulate it, was petulant. It bit into the air like an iron rasp. He was not heard in patience. People in the church stalls fidgeted and squirmed. It was as if one and all were shrugging their shoulders. When he called on them to look at their shame, visible as lice on the crucifix, they didn't raise their eyes, but looked away almost defiantly. He sensed their hostility.

I must not lose patience with them, he told himself. Human nature, he reminded himself, is very very weak. It was natural for his flock to relapse in this way. He must go out to them, as a father, in loving confidence. He stood at the door of his church, after mass, and tried to give each of them his personal assurance of his belief in them . . .

Person to person, some of them relented of their stiff attitude in church. But others openly rebelled. One of them went so far as to ask, how can we be sure, reverend father, that what has happened to the cross is a sign from God, and not an insult from the devil. Another church member said, was it really a good thing to be able to see one's sins in so dramatic a fashion. He wasn't speaking for himself, mind you, father — but wouldn't it it tend to harden people's hearts and make them brazen — just as a prostitute is turned into a brazen huzzy by the outward, open wickedness of her life of vice?

The good bishop shook his head. No, no, he said. We must take it as a miracle from God. If it is a miracle, how can it work for evil?

One of his priests ventured to speak to this question. The younger of the two (the one he loved particularly) observed that, if the result of the manifestation of lice on the crucifix did cause *more* sinfulness, then ought we not to conclude that it was, on this very argument of the bishop, one of the works of the devil?

No, no, no, said the bishop in anguish.

The younger priest held his tongue until the bishop had gone, and then observed, to the other priest, that "we must conclude this, mustn't we?" — "I don't know what to think," said the elder of the two.

The bishop however, received instructions from his superior, the archbishop, that it was plain, from the scandal of the "miracle," that the "miracle" must be adjudged "no miracle." He must therefore have the cross cleansed of the "miraculous" lice, which were, in all probability, due to some natural cause, and to be accounted for as some unusual but perfectly *natural* plague.

This intervention of his superior was perhaps brought about because some professors of science at the University had examined specimens of the infestation, as they called it, and had pronounced upon the nature of the insects making up their "sample," obtained with a genuine zeal for truth but in an unlawful way. All were such varieties of bloodsucking vermin as could easily be found in

Edmonton. There was no satisfactory explanation forthcoming as to how they occurred where they did in such numbers. However, according to one wag, a rough estimate of the number of insects on the crucifix could be made; and hence, a count of the number of sins committed in Edmonton.

Moreover, an analysis of blood taken from some of the lice was made. The reports about this analysis were conflicting. Not all the samples were said to be human blood; and more than one type of human blood was detected. It could not be maintained then that the blood in the lice was the blood of the Saviour, as the bishop was said to suppose. All in all, these investigations didn't completely prove the miracle to be a fraud, but they left considerable room for speculation.

With a sad heart, the bishop ordered the crucifix to be cleansed of the lice infesting it. What his hopes were, may be expected. He was consequently most despondent when, after vigorous disinfection, the cross was once more free of lice.

He went to his room and prayed, not for another miracle, but simply prayed — wordlessly he opened his heart in passive obedience to God. He remained in prayer for most of the night. When the next morning — it was Wednesday morning — he again went into the church, he didn't dare raise his eyes at once to the cross.

When he did so, he saw it was clean — as clean as the cleaning people had left it. He realized that what had occurred might easily be taken as a defilement of the church — that the church might have to be re-consecrated. The archbishop indeed had gently hinted as much in an exchange of letters.

On Thursday, the crucifix was still free of infestation. And so it was on Friday. And on Saturday.

On Saturday morning, the Edmonton *Journal* reported what had taken place in the church during the week: the cleansing away of the lice infesting the crucifix. Though asserting his belief in the sanctity of the bishop, the editor urged his readers not to draw hasty conclusions from exceptional circumstances. Perhaps, this strange happening might prove to be, not a supernatural event, but one of those many natural miracles that our age has provided, and its solution a feather in the cap, not of religion, but of science.

But when, on Sunday morning, the bishop, about to say mass, raised his eyes to the cross, there, lo and behold, were the lice clinging to it, as if it had not been subject to the activities, on the Tuesday before, of the vermin exterminators.

He wanted to cry out, then and there, Look, O ye of little faith, the lice have returned — your sins and mine have again been made visible. But he made no allusion to the repetition of the miracle, as he thought, or to the re-infestation of the crucifix, as most of his congregation thought. He learned that they thought so, as he spoke to them after mass.

They seemed to be daring him to assert that the crawling insect life on the crucifix was, in fact, a miraculous manifestation of their sins.

He held his peace.

By doing so, he earned the approval of his younger priest (the one he loved), who remarked to his brother priest that he thought the bishop had shown wisdom and discretion in maintaining silence in the face of the return of the plague of lice.

The bishop again ordered the exterminators into the church. But Monday, Tuesday, Wednesday, Thursday, Friday and Saturday — though they exerted all their efforts, the exterminators had no success. They were this time unable to cleanse the cross of its vermin. Nor could they find any natural cause why it should be infested.

They did spray the sanctuary and the body of the church with quantities of an insecticide having deodorant properties. The smell of the lice had become extremely unpleasant — as the younger priest said to his confrere, "God is not only making our sins known to our eyes, but to our noses." The odour of the spray which the vermin-exterminators used rather enforced the stench of the vermin (they seemed unable to kill) than eradicated it or covered it up. As one entered the church, a strong suspicion of violets made one's nose quiver. But this scent of violets quickly changed to a strong whiff of carrion. It was as if, in a flower garden, you were hit by an overpowering smell given off, say, by the putrefying body of a dead animal, a dead cat or dog.

Because of this smell, and for other reasons, I should have thought that there would have been no congregation on the following Sunday, but such was not the case. The fact is, an angry congregation makes a full church.

The bishop, for his part, flatly and without emotion (still calling his flock, "my children") re-asserted his belief in the miracle. He said that they were right to be ashamed of what had happened to the crucifix, but, though this shame was a good thing, they were wrong to think there was no way to end the pollution of their church.

The church was polluted by sin.

It could be purified by fighting against sin, and God had helped to make this fight easier, by showing them their sins.

The bishop was nevertheless conscious all through mass of the hostility of the people.

After mass, very few spoke to him, but one forthright, golden-hearted old woman spoke out her mind. "I think it is a miracle, father. But it is a very hard one for human flesh and blood to stomach."

"God will provide us with strength."

"It is a very hard thing, reverend father."

3

All that next week, the bishop reflected on what she said to him. He wondered if he had been too fanatical in his zeal to reform his flock. He recalled to mind how he had asked for the miracle, the wonderful vision he had had of his people, that first morning, when the miracle had come, and the unhappy aftermath. Was God judging *him*? He felt very despondent.

Little by little, however, he began to repair his morale. He chided himself for lacking courage, he blamed himself for lack of faith — he blamed himself, too, for not realizing that he must face a desperate struggle with the forces of evil. He also reminded himself that he had an ally in God.

After all, the bishop told himself, he was the shepherd of his flock, and the good shepherd lays down his life for his sheep. He himself must give up his life for his sheep, if need be.

By Saturday, a course of action shaped itself in his brain. That night, he again prayed articulately to God.

Thy will be done, O Lord — but, if possible, let the pollution of the cross with the sins of my flock cease — even if the lice could infest me — yes, yes, the shame of the polluted cross is too great for them — let the lice infest me . . .

So he prayed.

The next morning, Sunday morning, he knew that his prayer had been answered, there was no doubt of that. For he himself was covered with the lice. He was torn between thankfulness to God, and the bodily torment of the plague of vermin.

In church, he saw that the cross was free. As he heard mass being said, he began to wonder if he had the strength to undertake the task he had asked for. After the *credo*, he went to the altar rail, and again stood before his flock.

"By miracle," he told them, "it has pleased God to show us all, my children, how our sins hurt his Son. But here is another miracle. He will now show us, such is his will, how his priest is hurt by the sins of his people — your sins, my children."

There was neither joy nor reproach in the bishop's voice. He spoke in a factual manner. Having finished speaking, he divested himself of his clothes, down to the waist. Then he held his arms up above his head, so that all in the church could see how the lice which had clung to the crucifix, were now transferred to him.

He walked down the centre aisle of the church and back again, all the time holding his hands above his head.

Then he drew his clothes about him.

He felt, during the rest of that Sunday, and through the other days of the week following, that what God had made happen He had made happen for the best. There was, he believed, a great decrease in the number of lice crawling over his body. He was by no means free from the physical discomfort of them. The comforting thing was, the lice had decreased.

On the following Sunday, he once again experienced the joy he had known, in a surpassing degree, on the day of the first miracle.

It seemed to him that the people in the church were shining with a new cleanness — especially the faces of some of the girls and young women of the congregation seemed to be lit up with the light that must once have shone in the Garden of Eden, the garden of aboriginal innocence . . .

But, immediately after mass had been said, he sensed a relapse. He knew there must be some retrogression — his experience of human nature told him that. But he suspected from the great increase in the number of lice on his body that the increase had been disappointingly great.

Throughout the following week, the lice on his body increased. In fact, on Sunday, he could hardly bring himself to go to mass.

But he did.

And once again, he stood up before the people, and stripped off his clothes, and showed them his body covered with lice.

"My children," he began, but he got no further.

An unprecedented thing happened.

A woman near him interrupted him. "The smell, father" — this was as far as she got and stopped surprised at herself. "It's the smell of sin — it's your smell, my children," the bishop answered her.

A loud arrogant male voice took up the woman's complaint.

"I'm a Christian, but it's not sanitary for you to appear like this, father . . . you ought not to come into church like it . . ."

A chorus of voices took up the protest, and soon everybody joined the hubbub.

"You ought to be ashamed of yourself, father, coming to mass like this . . ." — "Stay at home, father, until you are fit to be seen in public . . ."

— "This isn't any miracle, father, it's just filth . . . . How can we expect our kids to keep clean and wash the backs of their ears and comb their hair, father, if you come to church all covered with lice?" — "Be off with you, father, you're lousy . . ." — "Go and wash, father." — "Take a bath, father." — "Wash yourself in Lysol, father."

"Shut up," a girl shouted out hysterically.

The bishop steadied himself on the rail of O'Briens's pew, and wrote with his finger in the dust — for the wind had filled the church with the summer dust, which hung over the city like a cloud, and, sifting into the church, made all the wood-work gritty to touch.

A boy's voice whined from the back of the church, "Go de-louse yourself in the river Jordan, father."

"My children," the bishop began again, "these are your sins . . ."

"No, they are lice, father."

"They look like lice, father."

"My children," the bishop wept . . .

"Off with him."

"Out of the church with him."

"Chase him out."

With the women, girls and children screaming denunciation or encouragement, the male sheep of the bishop's flock pushed out of their stalls, and, approaching their half-naked shepherd, began to butt him out of the church.

His priests ran to help him into the bishop's residence, which was adjacent. Once in, he threw his discarded clothing across a wooden library table, and then searched in the pocket of his jacket for a packet of cigarettes — it was a packet of Player's he had bought as long ago as the week before the *first* miracle. He hadn't smoked a cigarette since then.

He fumbled with trembling fingers at the packet. Approving this indulgence, one of his priests (the younger one he loved), reached into his own pocket for a booklet of matches, tore off a match, and stood waiting to light the bishop's cigarette. But when the bishop got his box of smokes open, he found the half-filled package swarming with lice. They clung to the cigarette he started to extract, and he pushed it back into the contaminated container.

"Have one of mine, father," urged the younger priest, and offered him a cigarette of his own.

"No, no — no thank you, my son."

"A smoke will do you good, father."

"I will have one of my own." he told his priest. And he extracted the cigarette he had just rejected, tapped it so that the lice clinging to it dropped back into the box, and put the cigarette to his mouth.

The priest lit the cigarette.

But the lice had crept into the tobacco, and the stench of burning insects made the smoking of the cigarette impossible.

The bishop butted it.

As he did so, an upboiling of emotion, a tide burning hot and freezing cold by turns, seethed through every blood vessel, every artery and vein, every capillary, every fibre of his flesh. His skin contracted under its covering of vermin. What he experienced was a recognition. He knew . . . at this moment . . . with absolute certainty . . . that he was picked out to be a martyr . . . and, too, he knew that his suffering . . . the passion of his martyrdom . . . was now begun.

"Lord," he said, "I am afraid. But let your will be done."

He stood up erect, a sense of glory swelling within him, and pulling at his stiff, slack, aging skin — a sense of glory made trebly delicious to his senses by the itching of the lice which clung to him and were sucking his blood. His skin was aflame. If only the world knew, he thought to himself — it was for nothing so sensually delicious as this, that men lusted after the caresses of harlots, and gave up their immortal souls for the embraces of adultery.

Yet it was an agony.

Embarrassed, awkward, his two priests stood beside him, not knowing what to do, or what to advise. The younger priest was thinking over a course of action. They were both startled when the bishop spoke to them in a voice of command.

"Read to me."

"Read *what* to you, father?"

"Read to me from the scriptures."

"Wouldn't it be better," the younger priest presumed to say, "if you tried taking a shower — I'm thinking of your personal comfort," he added, for he saw the look kindling in the bishop's eye.

"Read to me from the scriptures," the bishop ordered him.

"Yes, father, what shall I read?"

"From the last chapter of the Book of Isaiah," decided the bishop. *Sion deserta facta est. Jerusalem desolata est . . . quomodo si cui mater blandiatur* — but as one who comforts his mother. I will comfort you . . ."

He understood now, as the younger priest read to him from Isaiah — he grasped now with the firm-handed grasp of inner comprehension, the meaning of the phrase, *vicarious sacrifice.* He . . . God was going to accept him . . . as a sacrifice for his flock. Because of the shepherd's love for his sheep, the sheep would be saved — what foolish sheep they are! But this, it seemed to the bishop, at this moment, was the most precious of the truths of Christendom. With this imperfect coin of our lives, we can buy the lives of others, and save them from . . . and so perfect ourselves . . . Yet as he thought these words, he realized that he had never loved his congregation. At best, he tolerated them. Indeed, he had *despised* his flock, he had, hadn't he, in trying to purify it — make it what it wasn't? Now he knew the formula. He must offer himself. And God had accepted his pretended love for his people, as *if it had been a real living love.* Or was God showing to him his own worthlessness? No, that was an anthropomorphic idea. Rather, God was taking him at the word of his lips, and overlooking the empty hollowness behind that word — the emptiness of his heart. The bishop recalled the exemplum, the little medieval sermon anecdote, of Pers, the usurer. Pers, the usurer, had never done a charitable deed in all his life. But once he had flung, not *in* but *out* of charity, in anger, a loaf of bread at a starving woman. This act of violence had been reckoned — after the system of accounting of heaven — as a good deed to the credit of Pers, the usurer.

"Now let me be for a little while," the bishop said to them, adding, gently, "my sons." He went up to his room. When the younger of the priests visited him after a short lapse of time, he found the bishop collecting together his belongings.

"You are leaving us, father?"

"You have been making arrangements for me to leave you, haven't you, my son?" The apparent clairvoyance of the bishop disturbed the priest.

"Something must be done soon, father."

"Yes, my son. I'm collecting my personal things together. But I shan't, I think, have much use for them."

The priest bowed his head, and left.

4

Later in the day, the bishop agreed, with no fuss, without a single objection, to a proposal of his younger priest. It was that he should leave his see, leave Edmonton, and go into retirement. If he did agree — all the arrangements, said the younger priest, had been made. An unoccupied farm-house had been put at the bishop's disposal by a member of the congregation, on account of the great scandal the church was suffering. It was provided with bed, table, chest of drawers, other simple furnishings, and the owner wanted no remuneration for it. Nearby, there lived an old woman who had agreed to look after the bishop — she was unfortunately a Presbyterian, but otherwise of unexceptionable character. The arrangement, the younger priest had admitted to the older priest, seemed almost to be a providence of God. "But will he be persuaded . . ." the older man had wondered. "Ah, yes . . . that's our difficulty," said the priest whom the bishop loved. It had proved, however, to be no difficulty at all.

After all the arrangements had been made, there did occur *some* difficulty in getting the bishop transported out to his new house. No taxicab would agree to accept the lice-ridden churchman as a fare. No one in the bishop's congregation seemed anxious to transport the bishop out there — partly from shame, for no one wanted to be the person chosen to drive the bishop away from the fold; partly, too, there was fear of infesting the car in which the verminous bishop would have to ride.

Put to some pressure, finally one church member offered his car and his services as a driver. It was understood that the car should afterwards be fumigated thoroughly at the church's expense. If the driver of the car picked up any of the vermin on his own person, he too was to be compensated. Some simple precautions were taken. A stout white heavy cotton sheet was draped over the back seat, and another sheet was stretched across between the back seat and the driver's seat — so that the driver would be shielded as much as possible from infestation. Oddly enough, the lice seemed to prefer the bishop to the car or its driver, for none of them (so I was told) were afterwards found either on the driver's person, in the back seat upholstery, in the armrests, in the lining of the car roof, or under the floor-mat. "Isn't that miraculous," the driver said to the younger priest, who had been largely responsible for these arrangements. "Very remarkable," was the answer.

A fairly large crowd gathered at the bishop's house to witness his departure. The police were present, in case of trouble. But there was no demonstration. His farewells were much abbreviated. The elder priest offered to come and live with the bishop. But the bishop, with his eye on the younger priest, whom he loved, wouldn't hear of it. Both priests, he said, were needed in the church. A few intransigents from his congregation assembled a small group of children with fir boughs, which were to have been flung under the car as it drove away. But though the little mites waved their fir boughs faintly at him, no boughs were cast under the front of the car.

The crowd was rather sheepish. They knew the bishop knew they were glad he was leaving. So they merely stood about stupidly. Only one jaundiced teen-ager called out, with a voice of brass and ashes, "Come back, father, when you've got rid of the lice."

"That will never be," said the bishop, but he spoke to himself merely.

When the bishop had departed, the archbishop from afar caused the church to be re-consecrated, as he had beforehand decided to do.

5

The Presbyterian widow who was to look after the bishop discovered him standing alone in the kitchen of his new house. She had seen his car arrive, and came down "to be of use," she said. She was shocked by the fact that he was unescorted by friends, came, in fact, unaccompanied except for the driver, who, as soon as the bishop had alighted, and his few possessions been put in the house, fled down the road like a juvenile with a stolen car and with a few drinks under his windbreaker. Her good honest Presbyterian heart revolted at what she believed to be the treachery of the bishop's flock. "And they call themselves God's Christians," she exclaimed angrily to herself, "why, I wouldn't treat a dog so. The dirty Catholics. . ."

She tried to make the bishop feel at home and cared for. But the bishop was not responsive. The woman herself felt strange in his presence, and supposed he must feel strange in hers. As for his affliction, she resolutely closed her eyes to it. She did, however, take pains to assure him that there was a hot bath for him, whenever he wanted to avail himself of it. (The house had propane gas, and the younger priest had arranged to have a new cylinder of gas attached.)

After the bishop had seen where everything was, came introductions.

"What shall I call you, sir?"

"My flock called me 'father,'" the bishop told her.

"Very well, sir, 'father' it is from now on."

"And what shall I call you?" the bishop asked her.

"M'name is Mrs. McGinis. You can call me that, if y'like, sir. But the lads at the ranch, well, they call me mom, or mother . . . guess I am older than you, sir, if'n we took a count of our years."

"Then if you wish it — I will call you . . . mother," said the bishop.

"There's some lovely nice hot water in the tank," were her parting words, to which she added, very self-consciously, "father."

"Thank you, thank you," said the bishop.

She went away muttering curses against the Pope, Cardinal Sheen, monsignor the archbishop, and all Roman traitors — "leaving the old man alone, like this. The dirrty Dogans, the dirrty Dogans."

6

All day, the bishop's heart had been anaesthetized by inner misery. But as soon as the Presbyterian widow had left, his feelings began to awake. As long as his heart had been numb, he hadn't noticed the torment of the lice. Now that his heart revived, stirred first of all by the solicitude of Mrs. McGinis, and especially by the flowers she had set out for him at his table, desk, and bedroom altar, he could feel the agony of the lice. He tried to school himself not to scratch at his hands, arms, limbs, or trunk. But every now and again he lost control of his fury, and clawed savagely into his flesh, until the futility of scratching wearied his fingers.

He sat down at the table to eat the meal arranged for him by his part-time housekeeper. But as he reached for the potato salad, cold meats and pickles that Mrs. McGinis had left him, lice from his body dropped on to the plate of food, and though he tried to brush them away, they seemed viciously intent on getting into his food and contaminating it. At length, he got up from the table without eating. He made tea, but he drank none, for it too was spoiled by lice falling into his cup.

He took off his clothes, because the suffering was less when he was almost naked. He stood up, because the vermin were most bearable in that position.

He was almost caught in half-naked state by Mrs. McGinis, when she called later on in the evening to see if all was well.

After she had gone, he did eat a very little food, and drink a sip of tea. He lay down on his back on his camp-cot, and at long last, very late at night, slept a little. He couldn't pray. All he could do was to keep asking, out of his affliction, *How long, O Lord, how long?*

The next day, he tried taking a bath. But though many of the vermin were drowned in the very hot bath he poured himself, his suffering wasn't lessened, for the water made his skin more tender to the biting of the blood-sucking insects. He couldn't dry himself, because the chafing of the towel set up an intolerable itching. As he stood dripping onto a towel, he decided that bathing was a luxury he couldn't repeat. Anxious not to offend Mrs. McGinis, he was bothered by the state he left the bathtub in. As much as he tried to wipe it clean of vermin, fresh ones fell into it. Finally, he abandoned the task (— an odd fact this, considering that all the reports I have had of the matter suggest that the lice were attracted to him as if to a magnet).

On the night of the second day, he slept early and long. Next morning, he awoke greatly improved in his mind. He was able to pray; and he prayed for strength. When he had finished his prayers, he encouraged himself by thinking how glorious it was — his terrible fate. He had wanted to cure his sheep of their sins by showing them how ugly they were. But he was doing something better. He was actually helping those who couldn't cleanse themselves. He was taking to himself their iniquity. Certainly not in love — in wilfulness . . . but . . . God, he felt sure, was accepting his pitiful effort *as if* it was a true sacrifice. In desperation, he had said, let the sins of my flock come to me *as lice*. It was only half a promise, but God had insisted that he keep it. This was the thought which steadied his heart.

But later that day a relapse occurred. The afternoon was sunny and hot, the humidity in itself trying. He took off his clothes. He tried to pray, but couldn't. He shut himself up in his bedroom and wouldn't see Mrs. McGinis, who nevertheless called out to him, when she left, about the availability of bathwater . . . And why didn't he take a nice bath? He would feel so much better, she was sure . . .

Finally, his endurance broke.

O God, he prayed, *let me be rid of these accursed lice, so that I can return to my church. Don't punish me with them any more. I've had enough. O God, let me be set free of this torment.*

He fell into a long sleep.

In the morning, all the lice were gone.

7

He couldn't at first believe either his eyes or his skin, over which he kept running his finger. He immediately threw himself into a great tub of water, and bathed himself with wonderful enjoyment.

He was amazed to find that his skin was completely rid of irritation. He gave himself a marvellously revitalizing rub-down with the bath towel. He shaved, a thing he hadn't been able to do. Then, feeling like a new man, he had an excellent breakfast, drank two cups of instant coffee, and smoked three or four cigarettes.

When Mrs. McGinis came about eleven o'clock in the morning, she said to him, "Why, father, you look as if you'd taken on a new lease on life! — I see you've had a bath," she added, glancing in at the damp towels in the bathroom. "I told you it was all that was needed — it's the simple remedies that work. Nothing like soap and water. You see," she told him, "you have another nice hot bath tonight. Keep them at bay it will."

She insisted on changing his bedsheets. "But — why, you haven't soiled them at all," she said.

The next morning he took another bath.

He wondered how long he ought to wait before going back to his church. A day — or two days? He seemed so useless, just waiting around in the farm-house. He smoked cigarettes, given to him by the younger priest as a farewell gift. He ate his meals. He thought of how surprised his congregation would be, to see him again, so quickly. There would be no reproaches. It might be that he would love them better than he had done hitherto, because of the bond of failure between them — he had failed and they had failed. There would be mutual forgiveness. As he conceded his failure, as, putting it on like a new garment, he got somewhat more used to it, his need for the *community* of the church became more insistent. He must get back right away.

But at the end of the day, he discovered one thing: he *could never go back*. It would require just as much courage of him, to think out the new philosophy of life going back would require . . . the excuses . . . the new goals . . . that . . . Ah, just as much . . . as staying.

That night he didn't sleep at all. By morning, he found himself, with his new vitality, hating his cleanness. He bathed himself contemptuously. If only, he said to himself, I still had the lice — better the torment of the lice, than the emptiness of what I am now.

He didn't dare pray.

But, by that evening, he could endure himself no longer. *O God, he prayed, let the lice return to me. Forgive my weakness. Let the lice return, if it is your will, let the lice return . . . non sum dignus, domine, sed . . .*

He fell asleep. When he awoke, it was morning. The lice had returned. They were much worse than before.

8

So much worse were they, that before the evening of that day was come, he had again prayed that the lice leave him. In the morning, he was again free of them. He couldn't hesitate now — he mustn't play fast and loose like this. He packed his handbag. He prepared to leave. He would go back and love his flock, this would be the meaning of all that had happened . . . for him and for them, for they in return would love him too.

But when he was ready to leave, his decision wavered again. He unpacked his clothes, he decided to stay. He paced up and down the farm-house, into and out of all the rooms of it, like a caged tigress, her cubs taken from her and her dugs full of milk. He saw that he couldn't live in this state of irresolution, but it was a long time before he could once again bring himself to pray. It was early the next morning before he could pray. But then, a little before two-thirty a.m., he was able to. *Let the lice return to me. Let the lice return to me.* He then slept for an hour or two. When he awoke, they had come back. Back, and much worse than they had been on their second return. He took off his night clothes and lay for a long time naked on his bed.

The lice seemed to be multiplying. They were gnawing in his arm-pits — he tried to clean them out. If he rested on his back, they crawled across his belly. They crawled across the small of his back, if he lay on his belly. They got into his groin, and into his ears — he had already put wads of cotton wool into his ears, to keep the lice out, but they worked their way past that barrier. Into his ears. What lies, the thought shrieked across his brain, are my people breeding now?

The vermin crawled into his anus. They crawled across his scrotum, and got into the folds of the *glans penis*. What sodomy are they now committing, he cried out, as he scratched at his rectum . . . what fornication or prostitution or pimping or adultery am I suffering for now? The lice crawled over his hands — cupidity, cupidity, he told himself . . .

They crawled into his navel — across his teats — into his eyes — into his mouth, even . . .

When Mrs. McGinis called promptly at eleven a.m., she found him completely naked. But it wasn't his simple nakedness that horrified her, it was the sight of the true deformity of his condition, which, till now, had been more or less hidden from her. Good honest woman that she was, she shrieked with terrified disgust, when she saw *that*. All her fear of him turned into vituperation and reproach. "Why don't you do as I told you?" She threw the bathroom door open.

"Do as I tell you," she screamed. "Get in there and bath yourself until you are clean again."

He shook his head piteously.

"Look, father. You're going to obey me. Into that bath."

He shook his head.

"Goddamn you," she shouted, "do as I say."

When she found that he wouldn't or couldn't do as she ordered him, she banged her fist down on the table. "Very well, father. Very well. If you won't take steps to cure yourself, it's the last you'll see of me. Good-day. Good-day." She slammed the door, and went muttering to herself up the path.

The bishop knelt down to pray. *Lord, have mercy upon me, he murmured . . . but, O God, if I pray to be free of the lice . . . and I will pray to be free of them . . . have mercy upon me . . . don't ever listen to my prayer. Don't ever listen to my prayer. Let the lice be with me.* When he had said this prayer, he felt, for a moment of bliss, as if this resolution had carried him up into the seventh heaven of paradise . . . as if his martyrdom was completed.

He was able to say the Lord's prayer, and to make a brief act of contrition.

My God I love thee.

But then the torment started again. He kept shrieking, take the lice away, take the lice away, take the lice away. Then he would stop from sheer exhaustion. And then one thought would gnaw in his brain: what is the use of it? Isn't it all entirely useless, like mountain-climbing, aren't I like the mountain-climber, who only keeps on to get to the top, because he has engaged himself to get to the top? Again the bishop would moan, take the lice away, take the lice away. Then again his outcry would exhaust itself, and he would think, I'm like the Anaconda serpent which has swallowed too large a deer and can't let go of it because inward-curving snake-teeth have trapped both the snake and the victim. He was, the bishop told himself, the snake and God, the deer. He couldn't spit God out, if he wanted to. He also thought, these lice will purify me, but how can they help my flock, how? They continue as they were. Then once again the bishop would begin to keen, take the lice away, take the lice away, take the lice away . . .

Then his mind could think no more. He could only rage. Far across in the McGinis ranchhouse, they could hear him roaring. Mrs. McGinis put in a call to Edmonton, but could get no one at the church. When, however, the next morning, there was complete silence, the good woman again telephoned, and asked that someone be sent to the bishop's assistance . . . because . . . she was afraid of the worst . . .

9

It was at the eleventh hour that the bishop gave up the ghost. His friends, summoned on the next day, did not arrive at the farmhouse until the next morning after that. They saw then a third miracle, if the lice on the crucifix was considered as one miracle, and the lice on the bishop himself, another. What they saw was, out of the mattress of the camp-cot a thick turf of a marvellously green new grass growing. On, or rather in, this grass, were the remains of the bishop. All the lice were gone, and only his skeleton was seen, at first. There was absolutely no sign of any vermin, no flea, no bedbug, no louse of any kind.

Summoned by the Presbyterian-minded Mrs. McGinis, it was the police who made a second discovery. One was a constable and the other a corporal. The constable *observed* that death couldn't have been recent. The corporal, however, *looking* more closely at the bishop's remains, saw that, within the bony cage of the church-man's ribs, the heart and other chest organs were still fresh and new.

At this, the clergy were filled with fear, for they knew what had happened *must* be a miracle. "I'm afraid," said the constable to the corporal, "there has been foul play."

These policemen were to be present at the performance of yet another miracle.

The first to discover the bones, the younger priest (whom the bishop loved in particular), when he perceived what had happened, drew back. He didn't want to look at the miracle. It was there. He was convinced that it had happened. But there was nothing inside him to receive it. I am like a barren woman, he thought. The bridegroom comes into me, and I don't conceive. He smiled to himself, thinking what would a psychologist make of a celibate Roman Catholic priest using such imagery? He went into the bathroom. When he had made water, he put his hand to the hot water tank. It was, of course, warm. Then he went into the kitchen, and there he saw the carton of cigarettes, which he had given the bishop as a parting gift. He saw how many the bishop had smoked. And thinking of what he had *done* for the bishop (for besides the cigarettes he had out of his own pocket arranged to have the cylinder of gas attached, so that there could be hot water always available for the bishop's use), he was ashamed of *how little* he had done.

Pushing his way through the others who were still wondering at the bishop's remains, and pushing aside the policemen, who specu-lated as to the possibility of a crime, he flung himself down before the bishop, seized the bishop's hand, and wept, Forgive me, father.

It was then that the final miracle occurred, before the very eyes of the police. A great swarm of vermin appeared to descend upon the bishop's heart, as if to devour it.

Seeing this, the younger priest fainted away. When he had been carried into the kitchen, laid on the floor, and restoratives given, some one of the party noticed that the lice had consumed the bishop's remaining vitals, and that the skeleton was now completely free of the organs inside it.

But when they looked for lice, there were none to be found.

Four Times Canada Is Four

Walter Shramm had come to the conclusion that dreams have much more importance for us (and for the higher animals, of course) than Freud supposed. He would admit that some dreams arise from sex-repressions. "But there's much more to it than that," he would insist. He had a hunch — for he was too indolent to turn it into a serious hypothesis — but he had a hunch that the instinct of the higher animals (including man, of course) in some way operates through dreams.

How, he would ask, do birds come instinctively to build — just at the right moment, the — well, sort of nest that *that* bird does in fact build?

It's uncanny, he said.

But you're not going to tell us, Walter, his colleagues objected, that the she-heron's dream life is spent in reading blue-prints of heron's nests?

No. No. Oh, no.

That's more than we shall ever be able to prove, conceded Walter Shramm. But still, he went on, what causes the she-rabbit to pull mouthfuls of fur from her breast, just when she is about to litter?

Instinct? Pooh.

Or what causes the eiderdown duck to do very much the same thing? Instinct?

But instinct is a mere word to hide scientific ignorance. How does instinct operate in these creatures?

They begin, he speculated, to have a series of dreams, and taught by these dreams, they perform the appropriate instinctive behaviour. And this theory of mine, he insisted, makes a good deal more sense of dreams than ever Freud himself was able to do . . .

Shramm didn't follow these ideas very far.

But he did regard his own dreams as an expression of the instinctive wisdom of fundamental human nature. They became his instinct. He didn't follow it blindly. He was a man of considerable common sense, for an academic. But he found he could trust his dreams; and sometimes he would wish he had trusted them, more than he could bring himself to do.

When Professor Shramm had to face the arrangements for his sabbatical year in Paris, he followed his usual course, he worried. What really bothered the professor was what to do with himself. He had a year's leave of absence, with pay, from his university. Had he been a career-scholar, he could have followed some scheme of research and written a book. But he wasn't. Production scholarship was repugnant to him. He disliked even the jargon of the phrase, tasting as it did of diseased commercialism. If he was anything, he was a teacher. He would have preferred to spend his time in recreation. But he felt he *ought* to do something constructive, something which, written up into a report, and deposited on the president's desk, would look impressive. This is sheer nonsense on my part, he would say, yet he worried over it — not enough to get serious ulcers, but enough to start off these *instinctive* dreams of his. Anxiety dreams, perhaps. But out of them little by little he formulated his plans.

One night he dreamed of some French friends he had met years ago, before the Second World War. They had had an apartment in a large building in Paris itself, near the Opera, and close to rue Tronchet — or was it Boulevard Tronchet? It was the rue Tronchet. Ridiculous to think of writing to them. But as he worried whether to or not, he again dreamed of this very apartment building, which he hadn't as much as thought of for years and years — and he actually dreamed of Germainie Montondont, he dreamed in fact that he met her on the bottom floor, just as she was about to enter the tiny *ascenseur* and he of course was about to trudge up the five flights of stairs on foot — she had recognized him, and invited him to squeeze into the tiny elevator with her.

He glanced down shyly at his bulging middle-aged figure — but oh, that's nothing, she said. She scolded him for not having written to her, and the upshot was, he promised to write.

The very next morning (after waking early, rising, and breakfasting — and before his ten-thirty lecture) he sat down and wrote to Germainie's father. It took Shramm some time to find the address. But after searching about he did find it, air-mailed his letter, and received an airmail letter back very promptly — not from M. Montondont, but from Germaine herself. Her father had died during the occupation, she said, and she herself was now married, and, sad to relate, separated from her husband. Her name was now Mueller. She would be very glad to rent him one or two or three *pièces* of her apartment.

Three or four letters now passed in rapid time between them. For one thing, Shramm wanted a little more information and, besides, being naturally indecisive, he couldn't make up his mind whether to lease Germainie's rooms or not. Germainie's letters became more and more free and easy — even vivacious — she obviously, Shramm saw, didn't visualize him as a now middle-aged Canadian academic, gone to mildew earlier than European scholars, as Canadians do, unless they have administrative positions.

He was frightened, he was more than frightened, he was in mild terror. He couldn't be quite sure whether M. Mueller was divorced or not. But Germainie never satisfied him on this score. Finally, when she must have thought he had taken long enough to make up his mind, she wrote to him saying she had hoped he would rent her *trois pièces*, but that there were other offers, and that if he did think to engage them, he must let her know at once.

The day Germainie's ultimatum came, he had had a rather gruelling interview with a pretty but incompetent girl student, crossed legs, bleached hair, weak chin, and as far as Professor Shramm could estimate, no brains. It was about the middle of March. He had had to tell her that her chances of *not* failing his course were almost nil. The girl had broken down and wept. When he went home, he felt rather washed up. He took such episodes too much to heart. After a light supper of a boiled egg and bread and butter and tea, he had heated himself a hot lemon and rum, and gone to bed early.

He again dreamt of Germainie, and again he saw her as she had been years ago, a young woman, very *chic*, very much *femme*, of twenty—three or four years of age — which is not at all surprising, for he had known her first at that age. Only by an intellectual effort, though, did he manage to remind himself that she, too, had grown twenty-five years older.

She had wept in his dream. What her grief was, he couldn't discover. She had always wept easily. He had never of course been in love with her. But she had stirred romantic feelings in him, and he had allowed himself to think, long ago, that he had caused similar feelings in her.

In his dream, these sentiments revived.

He wrote to her next morning an aerogramme letter telling her he would rent her *trois pièces*. He felt positively gay. He knew he must soon make arrangements for the journey. He felt rash enough to telephone a travel agency. He intended to fly. He was to have gone down that very day to call on the manager of the agency, but his work had interfered.

He resolved to do so first thing the next morning.

Before going to bed that night, Professor Shramm tore a leaf off his block-calendar. It was one of those pad calendars you pull a leaf from each day. It had been given him by an old student, and besides the date, it had, for each day of the year, a quotation from Shakespeare. For the fourteenth — this was the number he peeled from the pad — there was the following verse:

If the dull substance of my flesh were thought,
Injurious distance should not stop my way;
For then, despite of space, I would be brought,
From limite far remote, where thou dost stay.

Professor Shramm could think of no reason why March 14 deserved this quotation. He read the verse for March 15. It was an obvious selection.

Caesar (to Soothsayer): The Ides of March are come!
Soothsayer: Ay, Caesar; but not gone.

It was then on the night of March 14th, and on the eve of the fifteenth, that Shramm had what he came to think of as the most unusual dream of his life. Yet at first it didn't puzzle him much — it wasn't so odd, as dreams go.

It was a simple dream. It consisted of a single dream image. He was, he dreamed, standing in front of a large-scale map of the world. The dream was as simple as that — indeed, he wouldn't perhaps have recollected it, if this single impression of a large map hadn't been unusually distinct and vivid, the sea intense purple-blue, the land-area intense reds, greens, yellows. The only odd feature of this dream didn't harass him until later: *there were two continents of America on the map, and Europe and Africa were lacking.*

* * *

Having no lectures the next morning, Shramm drove across the congealed North Saskatchewan river, a very bleak Rubicon indeed, into down-town Edmonton. He had no difficulty parking his small English car. He even found a piece of pavement without a parking meter. He entered the office of the travel agency he had telephoned. He was greeted by an official who asked him his wishes.

Nothing odd in this.

"Very simple ones," said Shramm, "for I want to go to Paris." He noted that the clerk's name was Mr. Brown — so a small card on his desk announced.

Mr. Brown laughed.

Shramm felt that he was being laughed at. But why?

It wasn't as if he had said, I want to go to Lyonesse or Camelot or some other non-existent place of legend.

"Well, where *can* I go to?" Shramm demanded rather weakly. Afterwards, he kicked himself for asking this spineless question, instead of insisting, right away, that he be given assurance that at the soonest possible date passage to Paris would be arranged for him, and no nonsense.

Mr. Brown took Shramm to a large map of the world. As soon as he laid eyes on the map, he recalled his dream of the night before. It was the same map as he had seen in his dream, the intense purple-blue seas, the red, green and yellow countries. But on the other side of the Atlantic was a *second* North and South America, just as in his dream.

"There are *two* Americas," was all he could say.

"Of course, there are two Americas," repeated Mr. Brown.

"There are two Americas?"

"Of course."

"Since when," asked Shramm, "have there been *two* Americas?" He spoke in the voice he used to address an inattentive student at the back of a lecture hall.

The question was received as if Shramm were something of a wit — Mr. Brown however made no comment. Neither did he laugh. He merely rubbed his hands. He rubbed his hands mirthfully. He kept on rubbing his hands mirthfully. Whatever is he rubbing his hands for, wondered Shramm. What's up? Is there some joke? Then he realized that Mr. Brown expected him to make up his mind about his tour. I *must* make up my mind, Shramm said to himself.

"Then . . . I'll . . . Let's see . . . I'll . . . well, said Shramm, "I'll . . . I'll go to New York."

He hadn't the slightest desire to go to New York.

"Which New York do you want to go to?" asked Mr. Brown.

"There are *two* New Yorks?"

"Yes, of course. New York One and New York Two. Which is it to be?"

Shramm was baffled.

"Which do you advise?"

"It is entirely up to you, Mr. ——— ?" said Brown.

"Shramm."

"It is entirely up to you, Mr. Shramm."

"There is no difference?"

"There is no difference," said the agency official.

"How can this be?" said Professor Shramm.

"They are exactly alike."

"Even to the Brooklyn Bridge?"

"Even to the Brooklyn Bridge."

"And the Chrysler Building?"

"And the Chrysler Building."

"And the Metropolitan Museum — it is exactly the same in *both* New Yorks?" expostulated Shramm, surprised at the thought.

"New York I is exactly the same as New York II," Mr. Brown said, evading the question.

Shramm was more than a little irritated.

He didn't like being spoken to in the callous-liar's voice of the radio or television advertiser. It is worse, he thought, than brainwashing. That at least implies a human if evil motive.

"There may be *two* Metropolitan Museums," he said. "But there is only one El Greco painting of Toledo — it can't be in both New Yorks."

"Both are exactly alike."

"Then one El Greco must be a copy." Shramm felt he had scored. He was sure Mr. Brown had never heard of El Greco, nor realized that the painting of Toledo was one of the great treasures of the famous art gallery. He was a little dismayed to remember that somewhere in Spain there *was* another version of El Greco's painting of Toledo. But Mr. Brown wouldn't know *that* . . .

"One must be a copy," he repeated.

"Yes?"

"Perhaps," said Mr. Brown, "But no one can tell which is the copy and which is the original."

"Any competent lover of painting could," said Shramm with undisguised scorn.

"I will also go to Boston," Shramm decided.

"Which Boston?" asked Mr. Brown sweetly.

"Does it really matter which Boston I go to?" countered Shramm. He felt sure he had Brown cornered.

"Yes," said Brown.

"Why does it matter which one I go to?" Shramm persisted.

"It matters in this way," explained Mr. Brown. "If you first go to

New York One, and then go to Boston One, that is one trip. But if, having got to New York One, you wish to go to Boston Two, you must first cross the ocean to New York Two, and proceed from there to Boston Two."

"Oh."

"You see?"

"I see."

"It's exactly the same if you first go to Boston Two, and want to go to New York One," added Brown.

"But I can see *that*," said Shramm. He was getting thoroughly fed up with Mr. Brown.

"In any case," he added sharply, "it's my intention, as it was when I came in here, to book myself a passage to Paris" — he spoke the name very firmly — "*via* le Havre. I shall fly." He eyed Brown carefully. But his little trap didn't work. He hoped Brown would tell him that if he wanted to fly to Paris, he couldn't go *via* le Havre. That was the steamship port of entry. Well, it hadn't worked, his little ruse. But it did stiffen his courage — the fact he had sprung it. He smiled. "I intend to stay abroad for almost a year, and I also intend to spend a large part of my holiday in Paris. Unless the weather should turn nasty, in which case I may spend some weeks in the south of France. In fact, I have my eye on Collioure." He looked intently at Mr. Brown's map. "I shall almost certainly stay at Collioure. It is a delightful little seaport, very close to the Spanish border, and, I am glad to say, unknown to most tourists."

Shramm noticed that Mr. Brown was allowing his face to take on the sweet unreasoning look of a parent whose child has announced an intention to set off and visit Santa Claus at the North Pole.

"Very well, very well, Mr. Shramm," Brown replied. "Would you please point out to me, on this map, where it is you wish to book passage to?"

"I will not," said Shramm.

He got up, and put his hand on the door-knob. "I don't intend to give or to receive any further geography lessons this morning."

Walter Shramm put the entire matter of his sabbatical out of his mind; he avoided maps, and places where he might run into maps, as if they had been the plague. At the end of a week, he had another letter from Germainie. He left it on the dining-room table all day. Then he put it into his sportscoat breast-pocket. He left it there for two or three days, then drew it out, and opened it. Germainie's message was nothing more than a very French exclamation against some alteration — *effroyable*, positively *effroyable* — that was being inflicted upon the tomb of Marie Antoinette just off the Boulevard Haussman. An alteration? Or was it being dismantled? Germainie wasn't very clear. They had walked there once, it had afforded a moment of some intimacy, and he would understand, she felt sure, just how she felt about the change — it was a desecration, a violation of time, a dishonoring of history, a wound to memory. He dropped the letter into the top drawer of his chest of drawers — the shallow one, where he kept miscellaneous things, odd cuff-links, widowed fountain-pen caps, and nearly empty aspirin bottles. But having pushed the drawer in and jammed it, he opened it again, and took out Germainie's letter and re-read it. He noticed something he hadn't observed before. She had signed herself Germainie Montondont. All her other signatures had been, Germainie Mueller. Good heavens . . .

The trance he had been in exploded into panic. He decided that perhaps he had better seek professional help — so he went to a psychiatrist who had once been his student. The fellow's name was Ronald Biltinger. Biltinger received him with great affability. Shramm found it easy to put himself completely at the younger man's discretion.

"I am having delusions," he said.

"Tell me everything, Professor Shramm," said Biltinger, with only a slight self-conscious bedside or rather couch-side manner. He had arranged Shramm on a couch which stood against the outer wall of his office. Shramm felt that the couch was an affectation. But he had to admit to himself that a carpenter has a bench, a barber a chair, so why not — why not, after all, a psychiatrist a couch?

"Delusions, Biltinger."

"Tell me everything, just start anywhere," the young doctor said to Shramm.

"I suppose I could sit up and tell you my troubles," hesitated Shramm.

"Oh, of course," agreed Biltinger. "As a matter of fact," he explained, "it" — he referred to the couch — "was an old piece of furniture they had at home, and thought I could make use of. Well, it does come in useful," he admitted.

Shramm sat up on the couch. "Are there two Americas?" he asked Biltinger in a tone of desperate anxiousness.

"There's North America and there's South America," Biltinger said dubiously.

"No, that's not what I mean," explained Shramm. "I mean, are there two North Americas and South Americas? Are there? Are there two New Yorks . . . and if there are, tell me why I should find this so incredibly strange. For I do."

Both men eyed each other for a long moment.

Does Biltinger despair of me, wondered Shramm — or, isn't he very sure of geography himself?

Biltinger however had gone to a cabinet and taken out of it a wax orange, a wax apple, a wax tomato and a wax potato. He put them on his desk. "I use them for testing children," he explained. He held the orange and the apple level with Shramm's eyes. Shramm flinched back. He wondered what was up.

"How many oranges have I got," Biltinger asked him.

"One," Shramm said.

"I have two oranges," said Biltinger.

"No, you have an orange and an apple," insisted Shramm.

"I have *two* oranges," said Biltinger, holding the apple up and jiggling it in his fingers so that Shramm could see that it was — unmistakably — an apple.

"But that is an apple," Shramm complained. Shramm could see

that Biltinger didn't like his insistence — as if it were in some way subversive, as if it might be true that the second fruit *was* an apple, but as if this could be the sort of truth that — well, to say the least, *unsettles* opinion.

"There are two oranges," said Biltinger.

"Two oranges?"

"Yes."

"But how?" whimpered Shramm.

"From the point of view of this orange," said the psychiatrist, "there are two oranges."

Shramm tried as best he could to submit to this therapy or diagnosis, or whatever it was. "But," he insisted, "from the point of view of *this apple*" — he pointed to the apple in Biltinger's fist — "there might be — might there? — two apples, then?"

Biltinger didn't answer.

Shramm thought, he doesn't like this inference — but is too much of a scientist to deny its truth. Even more, he is like a physician who, in the interests of his patient, that is, in my interests, would prefer to find more hopeful symptoms.

Biltinger still said nothing. He spent some time writing in his notebook.

Then, all of a sudden, the darkness in Shramm's mind split in two, and a storm of light whirled his thoughts about. Briefly, what he thought was this: from the point of view of Europe, there are two Europes, and, analogously, from the point of view of America, there are two Americas. It was an illumination both exciting and paradoxical. Yes, from the standpoint of Europe — and it was the older continent Shramm was interested in — there are two Frances, two Parises. He felt cheered up already, — though he jested within himself and said that no Frenchman anywhere in the world would admit to more than *one* Paris. Ah, Paris, he sighed, the one and only Paris! He chuckled. He felt thoroughly distracted in an exhilarating fashion. He bounded up from the psychiatrist's couch, enjoying the delicious confusion one feels after a hard game of tennis is over — all blood and breath and sweat. He grabbed the waxen imitation potato on Dr. Biltinger's desk, and perhaps even said something aloud, for Biltinger looked up at him from his notes, and murmured "What was that?" as if he hadn't quite caught a remark.

"*Une pomme d'amour*," said Shramm, waving the wax potato in Biltinger's face.

"*Pomme de terre*, isn't it?"

"No, it's a tennis ball," said Shramm.

"Tennis ball?" Biltinger was puzzled, but looking at Shramm, he felt reassured. "Yes, it's a tennis ball," he said, and laughed. He helped Shramm into his over-coat and went with him to the door. When they had said good-bye, the young psychiatrist started to pass a judgment . . .

"Yes . . ." asked Shramm.

Biltinger hesitated. "Good-bye," he said. But then he added, "There's absolutely nothing wrong with you, Professor Shramm. You're in excellent psychological health."

"Yes?"

"Excellent psychological health."

"Excellent psychological health."

"Yes?"

He repeated this judgement three times, reflected Shramm, after Biltinger had closed the door of his cubicle. Now why, Shramm asked himself, would Biltinger do this? It is no doubt part of the cure, he decided. But he *was* cured? He was confident — and what is sanity but confidence? He resolved right away to travel to Europe. This time he wouldn't stand any nonsense. Perhaps though it wouldn't be wise to return to the same travel agency. He didn't want to stick out his neck after trouble. He knew what he would do. He would go to Calgary. That's a very good idea, he told himself. I will visit my sister in Calgary. It was true that the thought of the dull two hundred miles by train to Calgary made a small dint in his optimism. I will go to Banff, he thought, trying to justify this excursion to Calgary. It will do me no end of good to have another squint at the dear old mountains . . . Sulphur Mountain, Tunnel Mountain, Cascade Mountain, Mount Eisenhower, oh, how right Wordsworth was! I can even take my skis, he thought — and get in a bit of ski-ing. Go up in the ski-lift, at the very least.

* * *

Shramm wasn't able to take the train to Calgary until the weekend. That evening — Wednesday — he wrote a brief note to this sister announcing his coming to visit her, and perhaps going on to Banff. He also wrote a much longer letter to Germainie. These finished, he decided to take a hot lemon and rum as a nightcap, but discovered the run bottle empty, so he heated some milk, there was lots of that, and took a hot milk and whiskey, and went to bed. He didn't sleep at all well. Finally when he had thoroughly disarranged the bed-linen, he got up, read, threw aside his book, decided to bring his journal up to date, and when he had done so (making no mention of the business of the map of the two Americas) he got himself another hot milk and whiskey, took in addition two aspirins, and tried to get to sleep. He dozed off soundly at once, only to be awakened by a four-diesel freight train in low gear with full throttle open — there was a railroad track just under his window. After another long sleepless period, he dozed off again — and was awakened by a low flying plane, which made all the windows rattle. It must have been about four o'clock Thursday morning before he really fell asleep. Then he slept very heavily indeed.

It was past nine o'clock in the morning when he woke. He was not at all surprised that he had dreamt of Germainie. It was a silly dream. All through it, he was aware of the fact that he was dreaming it, and all through it, too, he kept telling himself that the real Germainie must be much older — "this is the Germainie you remember, the Germainie of at least twenty years ago, the nineteen-year-old Germainie." But what was silly about the dream (unless of course his hypothesis about dreams was frighteningly true) was that Germainie had said to him, not once, but twice, "Look, why now do you not go to the French Lines office on *rue Scribe* and make your travel arrangements from here? I'll go with you, if you like." She had taken him by the hand, led him through the door, and as she did so, squeezed his hand significantly — he had blushed and then he had awakened.

* * *

When he arrived on Saturday morning in Calgary, his sister's husband was waiting for him at the station. "We've got a new car," he told Shramm. "It'll take any car on the road down a couple of pegs . . . acceleration is simply terrific. We're going to drive you out to Banff for lunch," he informed his brother-in-law.

"But," said Shramm, "I've first got to make arrangements for my trip to France."

"To France?"

"Yes. Hasn't Elsie told you about my sabbatical?"

"Sabbatical? What's that?"

"Year's leave of absence with pay," said Shramm.

"Oh yes, yes, she has, Walter," admitted his brother-in-law, "we think it's wonderful."

"And I think I told Elsie that my real reason for coming here was to make my travel arrangements?"

"Oh," said his brother-in-law. "Couldn't you make them in Edmonton?"

"Perhaps I could."

"Of course you could."

"It's easier to make arrangements for travelling to France," Shramm said, "here in Calgary."

"Oh?"

"Yes."

"Well, I shouldn't have thought so," said his brother-in-law. "But anyway, Elsie is waiting with breakfast now," he added, and steered Shramm to the new car, shining in the C.P.R. depot parking lot. But after Elsie had given them a hearty breakfast of grapefruit, cereal, bacon and eggs, Shramm insisted that he be allowed to walk down to the travel agency.

"But Jack will love to drive you there," objected Elsie.

Walter Shramm however held firmly to his intention to walk. He wanted to think, he told himself. But he said to Elsie that he wanted to breathe in the glorious Chinook weather which was blowing in from the mountains, Calgary air, all sunshine and champagne. In his heart, he knew that he was merely delaying the moment of crisis when he would once again say (but this time with the utmost firmness of soul) "I want to make arrangements for a trip to Paris."

"It's Fitzwilliam's Agency you want," Elsie told him, as he left.

"It's on Eighth Street, isn't it?" he asked.

* * *

The first thing that met his eyes when he opened the door of the travel agency was a huge map of the world. He averted his eyes from it. When he did dare to look at it, he saw that it had, like the map in the travel agency in Edmonton, *two* Americas. It was a bit of a shock. Still, he wasn't completely unnerved. For one thing, Elsie's breakfast of bacon and eggs stood him in good stead. He braced himself. He remembered, too, his visit to Biltinger, the psychiatrist. He now knew the answer. It was all a matter of two oranges — of the orange looking at the apple from the orangeness inside the orange, and projecting orange, so that it saw orange when it should have been seeing not-orange, in fact, apple.

A girl was speaking to him.

"I wish to go abroad," he told her.

"Yes?"

"No," he replied. "I've changed my mind. I wish to *return* to Europe."

"Where from?" asked the girl. She seemed to have only a rudimentary knowledge of travel agency business. Insofar as a teenage girl can be said to be human, Shramm decided, she seems to be human. She was obviously very inexperienced in the ways of salesmanship. She was, he supposed, occasional help. She looked as if she might be a student.

He was right.

For when he answered her question "Where from?" by saying, "why from *here*," and added, "This *is* Europe, isn't it," the girl stared at him in dumbfounded fascination, delighted as well as completely confused by this point-of-view-of-the-apple reply of his. "I will have to call my father," she told him, and smiled at him in a female smile which would have been appropriate, Shramm guessed, only if she had been subjected to profound erotic stimulation.

Her father was the manager of the agency.

When however she was gone, Shramm began to spoil this excellent beginning, and to lose his nerve. He wondered whether he hadn't better ask to go to New York. It might be less embarrassing, he told himself. By the time that the manager appeared, Shramm had made up his mind. Needless to say, he'd plunked for New York. He told himself he'd be able to see several new plays, for he felt he ought to give himself some reason for relinquishing the pleasures of Paris, the pleasure of meeting the long unseen, the much-dreamed about Germainie — the thought of her went through his mind cutting its way like anguish! But he'd arranged to rent *trois pièces* of Germainie's apartment, hadn't he? He couldn't simply couldn't, not now, *not* go to Paris! What sort of French had he, anyway, to explain to Germainie, so that she would understand, understand *parfaitement*, the plight, the dangerous plight he was in? Good heavens, his French vocabulary of words of *bafouillement* wasn't equal to it . . .

The manager was now confronting him.

He was dressed in a brown tweed suit. He had a short brushcut moustache and heavy creases which divided his leathery brown cheeks into puffy pouches on each side of his face. He had, Shramm considered, a promising tie. It was not made of shiny satin. It was a woven tie.

"You are going on a tour," said the manager. "And where to? Where in the world do you want to go?"

A jocular beginning, Shramm felt, and he nearly was rash enough to say, to Paris. But he merely answered, with aching feebleness of soul, to New York.

He might just as well (he saw at once) have said France or even specifically, Paris. The manager's daughter — who had been an unconscionable time getting her father, must have given him some information about the odd bloke — that's how she would think of him, Shramm knew, though what her phrase for "odd bloke" would be, he couldn't imagine. She would have said something about his unusual request and nervous perturbation. She might even have described him as an escaped lunatic — no, no, Shramm thought, she would probably have told her father that he had *personality problems.*

"New York?" the manager asked. The query was uttered in the tone of voice one uses to a child — "Ha, ha, you want to climb a beanstalk, do you, and bring back a bag of the giant's jewels, fi-fi-fo-fum . . ."

"Is there any reason why I shouldn't go to New York?" Shramm asked.

The manager immediately dropped his playful air. He became pure retired army major — he fell into logical reply, clipped, military, the adjutant-to-the-colonel, without any sir.

"Yes. There isn't any such place."

"No such place" — they both said it again together, man to man manfully admitting the truth, the perhaps painful truth, of the impossibility of visiting a non-existent place, New York. Shramm bit his lip, thinking as he did so that ever since he had decided on his sabbatical, a decline in his courage had set in. He was sure that the travel agencies were up to some skullduggery. They had sold, possibly, all their accommodation to Paris, and now to New York, and in order to push more unlikely accommodation, say, to Mexico City or Valparaiso or Santiago, they were coolly inventing the myth that Paris and New York didn't exist. The myth required a voice. The radio had devised this voice, invented it rather, and perfected it with long years of practice at advertising, and now the tourist agencies had adopted it — they perhaps even sent personnel to the radio stations to train. He knew the voice. Before he had decided on his sabbatical, three months ago, he had defied it — when he had gone into a department store to buy himself an L.P. recording of Respighi's *Fountains of Rome*. He had picked out a copy and asked the sales-girl to play it for him. "It is factory-sealed and cannot be opened," the girl had told him. He had shown annoyance.

People, said the girl, *prefer to have their L.P. recording factory sealed*.

It was her voice that had infuriated him. He recognized it for what it was. He spoke up to her.

"I, and most of my friends," he had said, "prefer to hear a recording before we take it home. And we are people, I presume?"

Most people prefer to have recordings factory-sealed, persisted the girl. She spoke in the sort of voice that an automatic coffee machine would speak in, if it spoke. It was the voice of a mechanical parrot.

The efficacy of the voice, from the point of *sales* is that sensible people recognize the voice's mechanical unconsciousness, and make no attempt to answer it. But not Shramm, before he had become involved in his arrangements for his sabbatical. He persisted with the girl, and managed to break through the machine-voice, to the human being he knew she was. He had kept at her, until she answered him in the voice of a human being, in a voice aware that a conscious human being was listening to her. She broke the cellophane wrapper, played the record for him, which, when he had listened to it, he purchased.

"You are perfectly right," the girl admitted, "people do prefer to hear what they buy — but we have to accept these factory-sealed packages. The recording companies are engaged in consumer education."

The Fountains of Rome!

Then he had been a man. In order to be a human being in this day and age you have to be a man.

But it was not the same Shramm now.

"Let us go to the map," said the manager of the travel agency. He waited at attention while Shramm chose a place of destination. He said nothing. He might have still been in the army — being inspected, perhaps, by some high-up brass, a visiting general, a prime minister, an English nobleman, or even royalty — stupidity to be endured in silence.

Shramm turned round to him.

The manager took a pace forward, "Well?"

"Toronto," Shramm said, catching sight of this name on the map.

"You want to go to Toronto?" the manager asked. He took out a pencil and notebook.

"I haven't exactly made up my mind," Shramm said. He hadn't, as a matter of fact, the slightest wish to go to Toronto.

"Which Toronto do you want to go to?" the manager shot at him.

Shramm wasn't caught napping this time.

"To the *second* Toronto," he said, feeling his answer was inspired.

The manager smiled wearily. He turned Shramm round to the map.

"Do you want to go to *this* Toronto," he asked Shramm, pointing with his finger," or to *this* Toronto (pointing) or to *this* Toronto (pointing) or to *this* Toronto (still pointing)?"

"Good God," said Shramm, "how many Torontos are there? How many Canadas?"

"How many Canadas in this continent?" the manager asked.

"There are four." He paused. "Simple sum of arithmetic," he observed, pointing to the map again. "Two Canadas in North America and two Canadas in South America. Two and two makes four."

"Two and two makes four," echoed Shramm.

"They did when I went to school."

Shramm observed that geography was becoming very mathematical. "Ah, yes," agreed the manager. "It is. And it defeats most people."

Shramm said he was rather proud of his own mathematics. "I have had some training in maths," he boasted. "I got as far as differential calculus. But," he confessed, "I didn't write the examination, even though I took the course. And after that year, I dropped mathematics. Because," he explained, "it was taking the flavour out of things — yes, such things as, well — quince and crab-apple jelly."

"Yes?"

"Yes," he said. "And the mystery."

"Yes?"

"Yes, and the glory."

"The glory?"

"The glory."

"Well," said the manager of the tourist agency, "that may be. But," he observed, "there is abstract arithmetic and there is practical arithmetic. In geography, it is only practical arithmetic that matters. Calculus won't help you with the nations of the world."

"No?"

"No — by the way, which *America* do you want to go to? Because, if you want to visit the *other* America, there are four more Canadas available, to reckon with. And four more Torontos. It is a little confusing," he admitted.

"Then there are eight Torontos?"

"Yes, one way or another."

"Eight Torontos?"

"Yes," said the manager.

"Toronto certainly must be a drug on the packaged-tour market," Shramm managed to say, as a sort of witticism — but no sooner had the words left his mouth, than the thought behind them bit into his mind.

"It is more than confusing," he went on with some asperity, "because at a travel agency of good reputation in Edmonton, I was told that there were two Americas, and two New Yorks."

"Ah," said the Calgary man, "that is because the Edmonton agency is an American agency." He paused. "But this agency, I'm happy to say, is Canadian owned, Canadian operated, for Canadian travel."

"In all the four Canadas," Shramm said satirically.

"In all the four Canadas of this continent, and in all the four Canadas of the transatlantic continent."

"I ought not to have gone to an American travel agency," Shramm hesitated.

"Please yourself," the manager said. "Some might consider dealing with an American travel agency — well, un-Canadian."

"But does it matter so much?"

"In travel it does."

Then, reasoned Shramm, thinking of his dream, and also of his theory that dreams are an instinct to guide and teach us, if we will only let them — then, if . . . if I went to the *French Compagnie Générale Transatlantique* —

"If I went to the French Lines Offices," he said aloud.

"I should certainly advise against it," said the manager of the agency with some warmth.

"But if I did," said Shramm going on with his hypothesis, "then I might be able to get to France?"

"You might . . . you very possibly might," said the manager with great dubiousness.

"Then," said Shramm . . .

"But where will you find an office, even a miserable sub-branch-office of the French Lines in Calgary?" the manager of the all-Canadian travel agency asked Shramm.

"Of which Calgary are you speaking?" Shramm said triumphantly, and turned on his heels, and walked out of the agency without as much as thanking the manager for all his time and trouble.

* * *

Back in Edmonton, Walter Shramm knew just what course of action he was going to follow. As far as making travel arrangements, he decided not to make any. What he concentrated on, was putting his affairs in order. He made a fresh will. He had a car to sell, an apartment to rent, his books to move out of his office, for naturally he would have to vacate it while away on leave. He was extremely shrewd in disposing of his apartment — he sublet it to a visiting professor of home economics whom he happened to know personally and who was a marvel of competence. He reckoned that a year of her occupancy might give an apartment occupied by a bachelor for many years, and gone rather dingy, a change of heart; and he also thought that, if he did — well, the fact that a woman had been able to bear his apartment for a whole year would be argument — but no, this was unthinkable, as far as he and Germainie were concerned, a renewal of an old friendship was the extreme limit of his intentions. He had to go through his papers too. He had to decide what baggage to take.

As for baggage, he decided to take very little. A few nylon shirts, nylon pyjamas, his eider-down-lined dressing gown, a couple of pairs of shoes, a raincoat with a detachable lining. If he needed anything else, he would buy it in Paris. His friends warned him that the cost of living had skyrocketed in France — but pooh, he wasn't poor. He hadn't bled himself white trying to follow a career of scholarship, buying books, subscribing to journals, going on trips, guzzling whiskey with important people.

The beginning of May came very quickly.

Then the day of departure arrived. He made his last minute farewells, and boarded the train for Vancouver, without as much as buying a ticket. This was all part of his plan. The train was almost to Edson before the conductor demanded his ticket.

"I haven't one," said Shramm.

"Ten per cent penalty," said the conductor.

Shramm knew all about ten per cent penalties. He didn't care. "Give me a ticket to Vancouver," he told the conductor. It was worth the extra money, Shramm decided, not to tangle with a ticket agent who had only a ticket agent's theoretical grasp upon reality. Shramm knew he'd have no trouble with the conductor — he guessed that the conductor would be a practical man too much taken up with the business of running his train to discover that there were two or four or eight or sixteen British Columbias. He would be ignorant of more than one Vancouver, B.C. And Shramm was right. Far from placing obstacles in his way, the conductor when he learned that Shramm was a university professor, procured him a sleeping compartment, so that he was reasonably comfortable as the train proceeded to the C.N.R. terminus in Vancouver.

A cab fetched him to the office of the French Lines on Hastings Street West. He glanced up wonderingly at the tall Marine building, around which curled a soft middle-of-May Vancouver fog. A small rain fell on his upturned face.

He went inside.

"As soon as possible," Shramm said to the agent, a young Frenchman named Duclos, "I must be in Paris."

"*Which* Paris?" asked Duclos.

"You a Frenchman," chaffed Shramm blithely, "and telling me that there's more than one Paris."

"But yes, there are many Paris."

"Then give me a ticket to Paris, France."

"It is impossible, sir," said the agent.

"Why?"

"Because, m'sieu, there is no such city as Paris in France anymore — that's why, M'sieu."

"Nonsense," said Shramm. "Look at this." He pulled a letter from his breast pocket. "Look," he said, "here is a letter I've had from Paris in France as recently as two weeks ago. It's stamped, Paris, France. This proves that Paris is in France. If any proof were needed. I want a ticket there," he added brusquely.

"Would you step here to the map, sir?" said Duclos, a trifle confused by Shramm's positiveness.

"Yes."

"Here," said the agent, pointing to Holland, "is Paris in Holland. Here is Paris in Switzerland. Here is Paris in Denmark. Here is Paris in Algeria. Here is Paris in Morocco. Here is . . ."

"I want to go to Paris in France," Shramm said. "F-R-A-N-C-E, France."

"But there is no Paris in France," said the agent. "Point out to me if you please m'sieur where it is in France, and I will make you out a ticket there. But if it's not there, I can't make you out a ticket to it."

"Gladly," said Shramm. "Look," Shramm said, running his finger about nine inches up the river Seine from the coast. "Here is where Paris in France is."

"Your pointing it out on the map, doesn't put it there if it's not there." Duclos shook his shoulders. "It is not anywhere on the map."

"Your leaving it off, doesn't mean there isn't a Paris in France, if there is one . . . it means — well it means that you've got a bastard map," said Shramm as callously as a homicide squad detective.

"Bastard map!" said Duclos — but then broke off. "Look, sir," he said to Shramm, "here is the French consul, he will confirm what I say. This gentleman," said Duclos to the consul who had just entered the agency, "insists that Paris is in France."

The French consul smiled patronizingly at the Alberta professor. But Shramm did not smile back at the consul.

"It is a very pardonable mistake, if I may say so," said the French consul. "But no, Paris is not in France. Not any more."

"Not any more?" said Shramm.

"*Malheureusement, non. Paris est non plus.* Oh," the consul admitted, "yes, there are other Paris. The exportation of Paris," he explained to Shramm in the low confidential voice the bureaucrat uses when he speaks off the record, "to other countries of the world has been one of our principal means of revenue since the Occupation."

"The Occupation," said Shramm.

"*Oui, m'sieu.*"

"But this letter — these letters, have all come to me from Paris, France," insisted Shramm, showing the consul his letters from Germainie.

"They're from one of the other Paris," said the consul.

"Pardon, m'sieu," said Duclos the agent, pointing to the letters from Germainie, all addressed in Germainie's very feminine hand. Shramm had flung them on the counter. "Pardon me, sir?", said Duclos, " — it is an . . . affair of the heart? Yes?"

Shramm blushed a very hot-faced blush, even for a fifty-five-year-old Anglo-Saxon bachelor.

"Then look," said Duclos, pulling a letter out of his pocket.

The consul shrugged.

"Well," said Shramm.

"They are," said Duclos, comparing the postmark of his letter with the postmarks of Germainie's letters, "all marked with the same stamp."

"Perhaps," said the consul very much annoyed.

"*Une affaire de coeur?*" asked Shramm sweetly.

It was Duclos' turn to blush. He blushed. It was a Gallic blush — a blush of such purity of joy, it put even Shramm's pure blush to shame.

"It is not the same stamp," said the consul, examining the evidence carefully.

"But certainly," said Duclos. "I have other letters here, also." He extracted them. "Look, M'sieu," he said to the consul, "you will see this small nick in the ring here — it is noticeable on all the postmarks. Therefore, these letters and my letters must have come from the same *bureau de poste.*"

"And where is that *bureau de poste?*" enquired Shramm.

"It is on *rue Tronchet*," said Duclos.

"In what city?"

Duclos replied in a human but shattered voice. "In Paris, France, *huitième arrondissement.*"

"I'm taking passage there," said Shramm.

"Yes," said Duclos. "I can get you — let me see — I think — a plane passage there leaving Vancouver tonight. I think I can — but you must be very discreet, sir?"

"On your word of honour," said the consul.

"Of course," affirmed Shramm.

"It would never do," said the consul, "for it to be known abroad that there is still any Paris in France — when we have been exporting Paris all over the world for the last ten years. You understand?"

Shramm said he did.

* * *

Shramm swallowed a sleeping pill just after the plane took off. He was sleeping blissfully. In fact, he was dreaming. He dreamt that he had arrived at Le Bourget, and that Germainie was there to meet him. She flung her arms around his neck and kissed him. "You don't seem a day different," she told him. "But you shouldn't have gone away." She tucked her arm into his, and drew herself close to him. "You are not a day older yourself," he told her. It was of course the truth, for in fact he was dreaming of her as she had been twenty-five years ago.

The Girl Who Lived in a Glass Box

1

Everyone knew that Orysia was a witch, and when she married Myrtil Paradachyn the drunkard we all knew we were in for further trouble. What was behind the marriage we didn't know. But we did know that she had caused plenty of trouble already. True, most of the things blamed on her, weren't of her causing . . . and how did we know, anyway, that she was a witch? It was one of the first questions strangers would ask. The sort of question we could only answer by further questions: how does one know a witch when one comes up against one — is there a certain test for witches?

The answer is, you can and you can't . . .

There is, and there isn't . . .

The real test of a witch is, if you aren't sure she's a witch, she probably isn't. But if she's a real witch, you won't be in any doubt about it . . .

The evidence that Orysia was a witch was so great that it couldn't reasonably be doubted. There were matters that were best not looked into, at least, not to prove she was a witch. Wasn't her old man a scandalous drunkard? And wasn't he a wide-talker? A blasphemer against god, and everything sacred pertaining to man and the devil? Was he ever arrested? Could the police of Edmonton get the goods on him? Of course they couldn't. Orysia knew how to cover up for him. She would turn a road into an impassable quagmire, as easy as sucking a tooth. She could send out their Model-A Ford light delivery truck plus the German shepherd to pick the old man up . . . she could do that, and if a driverless pickup truck running about your town isn't *prima facie* evidence of something spooky going on, I don't know what sort of proof that Orysia was a witch would be needed. If some rooky cop was foolish enough to start in pursuit, what Orysia couldn't do to the road between the Model-A light delivery and the police car isn't worth recording.

And in those days the roads weren't too good, even the best of them . . .

Yes, a driverless light delivery, going out on its ownsome, and picking up the drunken father . . .

And the dog was afraid of her too. Whoever saw a German shepherd much given to cringing? A German shepherd will face up to a grizzly. It was terrified of Orysia, that was obvious enough. Whenever Orysia called it to heel, it groveled on the ground with its tail between its legs.

2

Many of the old-timers (male) thought that once she'd been properly de-flowered, once she'd had carnal knowledge of a man, once this had happened, all her witch nature would flow back into the earth, where in fact, they said, it had come from.

But can a witch be de-flowered?

I remember a settler telling me that there is plenty of theological evidence to show that you can't de-flower a witch . . . but where he'd got this information from, I never found out. Perhaps it was like the common assertion that you can't hang a freemason, the explanation that before he came to hang, he was booted out of the freemasonry. If Orysia did get herself faced up to in a carnal way, she'd have to give up all her powers as a witch.

Well, I don't think she's any virgin, Mario the river-barge-man kept saying.

No, neither does anyone, Bill Pipe the plumber kept telling him. It isn't the act of sex which would make her give up the powers and privileges she enjoys as a witch in good standing, Bill Pipe said, she could have all she wanted of that sort of thing, without ceasing to be a witch. It's what comes as a result of sex, the side-effects of carnal intercourse, which would cancel her out as a witch. We don't know that she's had sex with anyone. We do know that she's still a witch. But, if she has had her bottom pinched by someone foolish enough to pinch it, and she conceives in the so-doing, and gets herself in a family way, then she would have to cease being a card-carrying witch-lady.

She's still a witch, said Butch Knife the butcher.

Edmonton can't go on like this, we can't go on having a *bona-fide* witch disappearing down every alley and be a real city, Bill Pipe said. Edmonton's got to grow up.

Bill's right, commented Benny Price, the garage mechanic. He really loves this city, and I agree with him.

She's caused us plenty of trouble, said Butch Knife.

You can say that twice-over, said Benny Price. How would you like to take over my wrecking truck?

What's eating you, said Bill Pipe. Every time you get stuck in your wrecking truck, you get paid for it, don't you?

Never get paid for the years she's taken off my life, said Benny Price.

3

But it would destroy the man that does it, these old-timers would agree.

Not unless he is so unfortunate as to hit the jackpot and get her pregnant, Bill Pipe insisted.

Sure it will destroy him, said Stinky Glass, the bar-tender. But someone ought to give her, someone ought to punch it to her, regardless. We'll have no peace till then, that's a cinch.

Sure.

Sure.

These talks about Orysia's curing were endlessly protracted, as long as beer and wind. The oldtimers gloated over every phrase.

Give what to her, they would chuckle.

Yes?

Give what?

The carnal knowledge of a man . . .

Oh, oh.

Yes.

It's what she needs.

But I won't want to be the man that satisfies her on that score, said Plankett the school janitor, allowing his imagination to outrun his wishes.

You'd never make it, said Butch Knife, in a keening eager little old man's whine.

Too much underbrush.

She's well developed. Chest upholstery's O.K.

Her boosums?

She has a wow of a rear bumper.

Yes?

It's chromium-plated . . .

Dazzles the eyes, even the thought of looking at it.

The oldtimers agreed that it would take more than a mutton dagger to cure Edmonton of Orysia; they all agreed that it ought to be done — by some one else, that is; they all never doubted for one moment that she was a witch; and one and all they knew that whoever did the deed of earth with her, would be destroyed by the dark knowledge he helped himself to . . .

Bursting over with sun-tanned manhood, none of them wanted to slake his wish on her in that desperate satisfaction of nature which they were equally sure the law wouldn't happen to see, even if done in broad daylight.

And though they would choose a victim-saviour, it was all words, mere words — verbal rape which no magistrate can put a man in the whinny for, even if justice had a mind to, which of course, in *her* case . . . since she was a witch . . . justice wouldn't dream of doing.

Oh no . . .

4

And now that she was said to be married to Myrtil Paradachyn (who next to her old man was the most notorious drunk in the town and its vicinity) there was too much fear of her, of her instinct for causing trouble, not to be apprehensive . . . how could Myrtil even if he went water-wagon sober for a year and a day measure her length bedwise with a bridegroom's tape measure?

He couldn't hope to, not even sober.

This marriage of hers, then, was a witch's trick . . . but whatever for, was an uncertain thing to decide.

The very talk of Orysia getting herself bed rights with Myrtil Paradachyn was dirty beer-spoiling scandal, to cheat the ale choruses of Edmonton of what they had come to think was their inalienable condiment — lager and darker brews.

They're hitched, all right, contributed Benny Price, the garage mechanic.

But have they consoomated their church bargain, asked Scotty MacDonald, the nightwatchman at Northern Flour and Feed?

They've consoomated it all right, said Benny Price.

I would not believe it, said Scotty, unless it were avouched by my own eyes seeing it.

Benny Price shrugged his shoulders up nearly level with the greasy crown of his head.

She's in a family way, he said in a whisper as solemnly certain as a freshly-opened grave.

I cannot believe it, said Scotty. Though I knew as well as her physician did she'd missed her times twice.

She's worse than that, said Benny Price.

But they were only married in October, said Scotty.

No, no, Scotty. You've lost your count. The water's been flowing under the bridge since late July.

It's froze up now, said Scotty.

Sure Scotty its froze up now, all right.

Then it's not Myrtil that's been the fathering of it, said Scotty, She's been faced up elsewhere.

Could be.

Mark my words, said Scotty. Sure as my prophetic soul, it'll be a monster.

So it might . . .

5

The beer-soaked voice of the prophetic soul of Edmonton, however, was, as usual, both right and wrong. We came at last to accept as true the fact of Orysia's marriage to Myrtil . . . that she was hanging out the signs of fruitfulness, was likewise a true fact . . . but that . . . when the child was born . . . it was a monster was the opposite of the truth. The child was perfectly normal.

Nothing wrong with it, said Benny Price.

That child, lamented Scotty MacDonald, will come to no good. Or I'll never trust my clairvoyant powers hereafter . . .

They say it's a daughter, said Bill Pipe.

Oh sure, it's a girl, said Benny Price, with the tone of voice which indicated that he had come to the conclusion that Orysia was never, despite all the unmistakable evidence to the contrary, a witch. But he only made a statement about the *sex* of Orysia's baby.

They're calling it Orysia, too, he said, somehow managing to imply that, since the newborn baby Orysia was obviously no witch, neither was Orysia its mother . . .

But this was too much for most of us. We couldn't help remembering all the undisputed facts of Orysia's trouble-making, or observing that the old man her father still managed to keep free of the law, despite his continued drunkenness, or giving some attention to the rumours that now, when the light delivery was sent out driverless to pick up the old man out of that particular ditch he'd fallen into, the baby was sent along, to give it an airing.

Has it been christened Orysia, asked Bill Pipe, the plumber, in a voice of mixed dubiousness and official chagrin at the possibility that a drop of water he hadn't given permission to, as an official of the city's water pipes, had been used to name the child.

She? corrected Benny Price. Well, he began to add . . .

My grandfather, a kirk minister in the old country, asserted Scotty MacDonald, would turn over in his grave three times, if I dared breathe a supposition contrary to the known fact that the mother was a witch . . .

She may have been a witch, said Benny Price. But if she has been consoommated . . . then she may no longer be a witch?

Do we know that Myrtil is its father? asked Bill Pipe.

I have seen it, began Benny. But the truth got the better of him. I have seen *her*, he said. But not close up . . .

Pooh, said Scotty. It's my candid opinion that the mother is still a witch, and consequently, its father is a certain gentleman by no means unknown in this town.

We reflected soberly upon Scotty's pronouncement. After all he was a night-watchman at Northern Flour and Feeds.

A certain gentleman, added Scotty, who loves the darkness and who has a very large interest in this city.

Edmonton, objected Benny Price?

You're mistaken, he told Scotty. She's not a witch . . . and the baby . . .

6

But, despite Benny Price's opinion to the contrary, Orysia — Mrs. Orysia Paradachyn — *was* a witch . . . well, she mayn't have been a Presbyterian minister's idea of a witch, I mean, riding about on a broom, and wearing a steeple hat . . . but if she wasn't Scotty MacDonald's idea of a witch . . . yet . . . nevertheless, she was most certainly a witch . . .

I myself have seen her light delivery travelling about the rural roads without a visible driver. . . . I have seen this not once, but dozens of times . . . I couldn't have been mistaken . . . I did see a driverless car . . . and I'm sure it was Orysia's . . . I never dared try to overtake it, of course. . . . after all, what would you do? I mean, if you saw a light delivery travelling at a good lick . . . thirty or thirty-five miles an hour on lanes which were little more than road allowances . . . and proceeding along them without a driver? You'd give it a wide berth? That's what I did . . .

But what completely convinces one that Orysia was a witch was her behaviour to her baby daughter.

I am referring, of course, to the glass cradle.

Who made the baby girl the glass cradle? I can't tell you that . . .

perhaps Myrtil made it, under his wife's supervision . . . or perhaps *she* herself made it . . . after all, she was pretty skilful with her hands . . . as a woman who runs a sort of ranch must be, nowadays . . .

Not that the idea of the glass cradle is so strange . . . for Orysia — Mrs Paradachyn — was a doting mother . . . and it is barely conceivable that a mother who completely dotes on her baby might be so taken up with the idea of the fact of her child . . . and it was a beautiful child . . . that she wanted to have it on view . . . always. I remember, too, that her husband was a total zero . . . he meant nothing, less than nothing to her . . . No, the glass cradle isn't more than fantastic . . . perhaps the glass cradle doesn't prove Orysia was a witch . . .

What does prove the witch, is the glass cradle . . . and then . . . the glass box . . .

I suppose many mothers . . . and perhaps some fathers, too . . . have wanted to shut their children up in a glass box . . . it is natural for the parents of beautiful children to want to expose them to the admiring glances of all and at the same time to preserve them . . . to shelter them . . . to *glass* them off, as it were . . . from the world?

But though many might want to put their baby daughters in glass boxes, who but a witch could actually achieve such a wish? There was, as I remember it, something uncanny about the glass cradle, even. You know what a child does to a mirror? Marks it all up. Leave your three-and-a-half-year-old son in your car while you slip into a grocery store for a tin of ground meat for the baby, and what happens to the glass of your car? It gets all smeary, as if someone had rubbed a slice of bread-and-butter butter side up over the glass panes?

This never happened to the glass cradle.

Something unnatural in this fact . . . but in itself it is nothing compared to the glass box Mrs. Paradachyn made her daughter wear. . .

You mean to tell me you haven't heard of Orysia's glass box?

No wonder you don't completely credit what I've said about her mother's being a witch.

And was Orysia, daughter Orysia, a witch too?

A natural question . . . but no, the child seems to have been a completely normal child . . . except for an unusual upbringing . . . except for the glass-box. It made a great deal of difference, for you can't go through life wearing a glass-box, and not be changed. . .

But didn't people object to having a child imprisoned in glass living in their midst?

They never saw the glass box. In one respect, it was quite unusual. It was completely invisible.

And this fact alone proves that Mrs Paradachyn was a witch? Doesn't it?

7

For over a year Chassa had been trying to tell Orysia *something* and Orysia had been trying to listen, and yet she had always changed the subject, just as it seemed to be on the point of being opened. But whenever there was a silence, she would remind Chassa. You've broken your promise. . .

What promise?

You know what promise, Orysia teased him.

The *something*, Chassa prompted her.

Yes.

I want to ask you something, Orysia.

Yes? She pressed her cheek against the glass side of the box, and swerved her eyes at him and away from him.

Will you answer me Orysia?

No.

No, you won't.

Why won't you?

Because you won't.

Won't what, Chassa asked her with a mixture of eagerness and weariness in his eyes. As if he were weary of being eager. She detected the weariness at once, for, despite all her casualness, she watched him like a hawk, sifting out every the least shadow of his moods.

She pouted, pressing her elbows against the glass.

Because, she protested, you won't ask me the *something* you promised to ask me.

Shall I ask it, right now?

You won't, complained Orysia. You'll ask me something else.

There had been quarrels, ridiculous, when you realize that after all they were mere friends, and far from having reached anything like a lover's understanding, had, each of them wanted to involve each other in endless mummy-cloth wrappings of mystery . . . as if there were no future, as if both of them were futureless, and as if the now, the moment that was stretching out into weeks, months, into the second year after they'd met, only existed to hide from each other a past, on each side, which mustn't be opened. And yet perhaps some sort of understanding, there was — even from the start. As if their whole relationship had been intuited, entire, from the first exchange of eyes.

Orysia's best friend, Sophie Telluren, had introduced them. He's on the look for a wife, Sophie had whispered to Orysia. You can have him, if you want him. No, said Orysia. I shall never marry. Sophie looked at Orysia, thought of Orly, Orysia's witch-mother, and shrugged her shoulders.

The truth of the matter was, Sophie was looking for a husband.

What, Sophie said to Orysia, what will you tell Mother Orly if he asks for your hand in marriage, right away?

He won't, said Orysia.

Oh yes he will, Sophie said scornfully, as if she herself had been subject to this sort of annoyance already.

8

The witch's baby daughter who had been raised in a glass cradle and taught to wear a glass box, and made to promise she would always wear it, was then a girl of between seventeen and eighteen years of age.

He's yours if you want him, Sophie told Orysia. Sophie was a wise girl. The truth of the matter was that Sophie herself wouldn't have minded a bit having the refusal of Chassa . . . but Sophie was wise . . . she had seen from the beginning the impact that Orysia had made upon Chassa.

I'm nineteen, Orysia had lied to Chassa.

It's a nice daughterly age, said Chassa.

No, no, it's not, said Orysia. Fifteen is the maximum for daughters.

You mean that, asked Chassa.

Yes, yes.

You really mean it? he had persisted.

Because . . .

Because what?

Because there's *something* I want to tell you. Chassa paused. You do mean it . . .

Mean what?

You mean . . . what you say when you say, fifteen is the . . .

Maximum age for daughters, prompted Orysia.

Yes.

Of course I mean it, said Orysia. But, she added, for daughters in general.

For you? Chassa asked bluntly.

Me? Oh, I'd have to think. But I do mean it, for daughters in general.

But what was the *something*?

The something, queried Chassa.

Yes.

You said you had something to tell me.

The question, persisted in, had seemed to Chassa to be an invitation to accelerate *things*, and, though he was surprised at the speed at which *things* seemed to be proceeding, and wasn't at all sure where they were proceeding to, he found himself saying, "something to ask you, Orysia."

He put out his hand by way of gesture, and Orysia, fearful that he would knock his fingers against the glass side of the box she was in, shuddered, no, and knocked herself so sharply against the inside of the glass box, that part of her exclamation was a cry, suppressed as much as possible, of pain. Simple physical reaction to pain . . .

He was silent.

He was morbidly silent. It was, she thought, as if he had asked his "something," and it had been an ordinary lover's something — or the ridiculous something of a man . . . well, getting on in years, who, perhaps . . . as Sophie had estimated, might be looking for a wife — as if it had been something of that sort of a something, and she had said, bluntly, no.

Though it was, Orysia realized, what she would want herself to say to him, if he had crudely asked her hand in marriage. So soon after they had met. Even though there had been no glass box, no witch mother, no need for any explanations.

It was what she would have to say.

No.

But now his silence was making the everlasting glass of the box seem very cold against the bare flesh of her arm, and against her thighs and side, which after all, had only a few wispy layers of clothing between them and the glass.

She wasn't, she realized, even sure of his last name. But, she thought, perhaps, in reality, when one is in reality, things happen in this sudden, odd way.

Chassa, she began.

Yes?

I . . . I.

Yes?

But I can't possibly tell you, she said. I can't . . . and you must realize why.

Because it might hurt *me*?

Hurt you, she had asked in surprise.

Yes.

No, she said — because it would dreadfully embarrass me.

Embarrass you? Why?

She hesitated. Well, she said, I wasn't saying no to the something . . . you were going to ask me.

Then . . . you were saying yes?

No, no, said Orysia feeling she had been outwitted. How could I, she asked in the most ordinary voice she could muster, answer at all, before I knew what the question was about.

She waited. But he said nothing. She thought, he's not sure of me. And the glass box told her, now's your chance to make good your escape.

She obeyed it.

Take me home, she said to Chassa.

But when he started to obey her, she defied the glass box. Leaning tight up against the glass, she reached out her arm, and touched him.

By a round-about way, she said. Unless you are in a hurry?

9

If it had been anyone else in the world but Chassa, Orysia thought, she would long ago have been forced to decide. But then she would have been compelled . . . well, she would have decided in favour of the glass box. He was the timidest of lovers . . . and yet tough and persistent as couch-grass, or, she thought, that grass they use to bind dykes with . . . very little earth it needs, yet it can live and grow in the force of the teeth of a raging sea. Its botanical name being . . . Chassa . . . For a long time she had been resolving each time she went out with him, that it was the last. But she always relented. It is so difficult to jilt someone whom one hasn't really accepted — when there is no understanding — and yet binds one so that something more than simple goodbye would be needed, a formal refusal, at the very least. She should have been able, women-wise, in the manner of a Sophie Telluren, to use this very sliding-from-day-to-day unsatisfactory relationship as her excuse. But the fact of the matter is, she wanted to have certain knowledge, she had allowed herself to become so involved in Chassa that she had to have certain knowledge that, but for the impediment of the glass box, she could have Chassa, or at least the refusing of him. She realized this desire was unfair, unkind. But she blamed it on the glass box. That she must accept. But now already they had begun to quarrel regularly, and since, very often, she was the cause of the irritation — again she excused herself and blamed the glass box — she felt bound to show him more than usual concern — a sort of tenderness — in order to patch matters up, before there was an open breach. Despite the glass box, in the teeth of the glass box, she refused to make her exit at the height of a quarrel.

10

It was the glass box which caused their very first quarrel. She had long ago got used to carrying it about with her, wherever she went, so long ago that now she never even noticed its weight. She had had to adjust her bearing to it, had to hold herself in a certain way — just as Zulu women have to hold themselves unusually erect in order to support the jars of water and other burdens they carry on their heads. She of course, unlike the African porters, was inside her burden. But the weight and difficulty of it introduced a fascinating characteristic tension into her poses. And since she was an exceedingly attractive wench, even before Chassa existed as a motive for being attractive, what might have been merely unusual or at the most bizarre in her posture, became utterly fascinating. She had always detested Myrtil her father, so that the fact that she had his nose, eyes, mouth and colouring displeased her intentionally, and though what was handsome in him went handsomer still in her, she played it down.

That is, until she saw the effects her looks had on Chassa. The oddness she got from the glass box had won him. But in the flush of this victory, she forgot all her antipathy to Myrtil, suddenly discovered that the nose, eyes, mouth and colouring he had given her were assets, and played them up. She taught herself to use the glass walls of her box to help her poses . . . when before Chassa she had only contrived to get along with it as a burden. But now that she was in love or at least considering the difficulties of being in love with Chassa, she discovered like a born artist the supreme usefulness of a containing frame . . . even if an invisible one. It was something for her to smile out of, or rage against, or retreat from.

You were going to ask me something, she reminded Chassa for the thousandth game of asking, refusing and avoiding.

You are as beautiful as a witch, Chassa had said.

No, she had shrieked at him.

He couldn't understand what was wrong with her. The fact is, no other word in the entire language could have mortified her more. He lectured her about the root meanings of charm, fascinate, and witchery, but nothing he said could make the word witch acceptable. Nor could she tell him what was wrong with the word, or that it was that word which had jarred her.

Don't ever use that word in my hearing, she had stormed.

What word, Orysia?

That word, she had answered, still angry but a little frightened by the effect her temper had had on Chassa.

Chassa hadn't realized what word he had used. And of course she never told him.

11

It was at the moment of crisis when she had at last admitted to herself that she couldn't bear to live without Chassa, that he himself discovered the glass box. The way he had accepted it was a relief beyond happiness to Orysia. It was an absolute miracle, apart and in addition to the miracle of meeting Chassa, Orysia thought, that despite his learning about her glass box, he should still put up with her, and it. Put up with — she corrected herself, for she had almost used the terrible word, love.

She had decided.

She would marry Chassa, if he would ask her. And if necessary, she would ask him to ask her, or at least, make it impossible for him, if he did care for her, not to admit the fact.

When she didn't examine the evidence too strictly, she rather supposed he did love her. No, no, she said, I can't go on like this — I must find out for certain.

But first of all, she knew, she would have to tell Mother Orly that the glass box was no go.

Not any longer.

It was then that she coolly opened the lid of the box, and left it.

She hadn't supposed it could be so easy a thing to do.

She got half-way across her bedroom, and then turned back to look at the box. It wasn't there. But then she remembered. Being within the box, and constantly aware of its envelope of glass, its invisibility was nothing to her. But now that she had stepped out of it, she was surprised that she herself couldn't see it. It was as invisible to her, as to others. She hurried back to feel where it was. She located it. Then got into it, to assure herself she could. Then she vacated it a second time.

She moved cautiously about the room.

She stretched out her arm, then stood on tip-toe, then on one leg, then crouched down on her haunches, and, pivoting on her heels, twirled her body round and round, until she began to feel giddy.

No, Chassa, she said out aloud, as if she were reluctantly accepting him; then she flung herself out on her bed. Having slept for years in the glass box, the bed-clothes felt voluptuously nice and wrong. She put out her hand to the other side of the bed, to feel what it would be like to feel Chassa's body there.

She laughed, or rather her whole body laughed at her, to think that she had been so silly as to have anything to do with the utterly unthinkable glass box, standing empty on the other side of the bedroom. She — or rather her body decided it was, just for once, going to have a good stretch. And she or rather it threw backward her hands above her head and pushed downwards and outwards leg, foot and toes, as if she were trying to thrust toes and fingers into the four corners of the earth.

There was nothing indecent about this stretching . . . not even virtuously indecent . . . for she was clothed in household shirt and slacks. There was no one there to see, except herself and the glass box.

Nor was there anything exhibitionist about the elastic reflex kicking her heels so far up over her head that her loosely fitting denim slacks strained against their contents. It was like the baby girl's delight in its new muscles . . . this reaction against the prison of the glass box.

But suddenly she dissolved into an unearthly shriek.

Uah . . .

There, in the doorway and framed by her kicked-up legs, which had suddenly become unspeakably obscene, stood Mother Orly. Orysia waited for something to happen. Then, thinking that nothing proves Mother Orly a witch more than her coming in on me like this, Orysia allowed herself to fall back limp on her bed.

The bed clothes seemed wicked.

But Mother Orly said nothing. She merely moved a sharp step closer to the bed.

Orysia jumped from the bed and with one foot in front of the other and with her arm crossing her brow, cringed aggressively before the witch . . .

In peasant melodrama.

The daughter's posture of fear somewhat mollified the witch mother.

Don't be afraid, she said. At your age I can't beat you any longer.

She paused.

I'm not even going to order you to get back into the glass box.

She paused again.

Why should I get back into it, Orysia broke out defiantly.

Why, mocked the witch.

Yes, why, pleaded Orysia.

Because, prophesied the witch, far worse things than beatings will happen to you.

Such as, defied Orysia.

That, taunted the witch.

Orysia blushed. Oh *that*, she said as nonchalantly as possible. I was by myself, she excused *that*.

I see everything you do, the witch said, and vanished.

12

Orysia had sulked back into her glass box, and then gone to phone Chassa, to tell him she wouldn't after all be able to see him that evening, as arranged.

But on hearing his voice and sensing his concern, she at last changed her mind — if, she said, he would put up with her. She hadn't wanted to inflict her miseries on him, that is all. . .

Later, on the way out to meet Chassa, she met up with Mother Orly.

Mother Orly was less angry, now that she saw Orysia was again glassed up in her box.

Don't you ever leave it again, she commanded Orysia, but the voice was only half mother tyranny — it was more than half passionate imploration.

And why not, thought Orysia, though she said nothing.

Promise me, said the witch mother.

I have already, said Orysia evasively.

I see, began the witch mother.

What do you see, said Orysia lightly.

That you intend to break your promise. I see it, I see it, moaned the witch.

No, lied Orysia. But, she said, trying to excuse her escapade of the afternoon. I had fearful cramps.

You could have taken aspirins, said the witch mother.

I did.

Well, you won't have them, if you don't go out with men, said Mother Orly.

I've always had them, insisted Orysia. She knew Mother Orly knew she was defending her friendship with Chassa. Some months, she added, I've thought I was going to die. The past few months they've not been nearly so bad.

Going with men won't help them, said the witch.

Perhaps not, said Orysia.

She poised the glass box high about her, and rushed out of the door to Chassa. She moved so quickly that the air whistled against the hurrying glass. Was, she asked herself, the glass box, the house law of the glass box, merely the equivalent of the religion other girls have to endure? Was it, she wondered, merely an excuse to permit the witch mother to tyrannize over her? If it had not been the glass box, would it have been some other, some other perhaps equally irrational snaffle?

But how silly the glass box was!

It was simply ludicrous, she thought, as she made it careen against the air, to have to endure it. Were human beings not only mad as individuals, as Myrtil was mad? Was the human species mad as an entire species? How ridiculously she and Chassa were behaving, if they both wanted each other, if it were a matter of the mating instinct or even if love were more than that — why had it all been so delayed? Delightfully protracted, she admitted, but wasn't it insane to get pleasure out of frustrating each other? Why were they so afraid of each other — yet it wasn't that . . . they were really afraid of other people, and these, were they nothing but manufacturers of glass boxes? Were human beings like a race of horses, which, over centuries, had been broken to bit and spur, so that when they were at last free, they had to go on needlessly insisting that all good horses wear bit and bridle?

The glass box!

Were we all, one and all, busy putting other humans into glass boxes?

And Sophie Telluren, when she scorned me for not knowing anything about painting, Orysia wondered, was she really turning art into a glass box?

13

You're cold, Chassa had said. I can see you're cold, Chassa had observed. Orysia, he added, you look as if you were in a glass box!

Glass box, she shuddered. And he had put out his hands to comfort her . . . though she had tried with all her might to withdraw it or at least to distract him, he had persisted, and found out . . . the glass box.

He at once began to explore it.

Don't, don't, don't, she had said over and over again. But though she pleaded with him, he had most cruelly run his hands over its dimensions.

You are *in* a glass box, he said.

No, no, no, I'm not, I'm not, she had sobbed.

I will soon get you out of it . . . poor poor little Orysia, he had comforted her . . . the wanting to comfort her . . . the reassuring assertive competence of his voice . . . *I will soon have you out of it . . .*

Will you, she had broken down and said.

Do, do, do, she had whispered. And yet, though she could have left it easily enough, as he struggled with the invisible glass unsuccessfully, she grew fearful of the promised freedom. No, she said. You can never free me from it. If you want me, you must accept my glass box with me.

It was hysterical of her.

He didn't try to answer her. I will soon get you out of it, he insisted.

Can you, she said, dubiously.

Yes.

But wait a minute, he commanded her sharply.

I am waiting.

I've almost undone it. Don't twist about so.

I am waiting. Waiting. Waiting. Her voice had now become a small child's voice, to tease him with.

Waiting.

Waiting.

Waiting.

Bless you, he grumbled at her — but then: I've done it. It's open. You're free . . . now kiss me, Orysia . . .

It was true.

It was unbearably true, he had found out the secret of the box. It was open.

Open.

The glass box was open.

Shut it up, she said.

Get out of it, he told her.

No.

I mean it, he assured her.

No.

Very well — if you won't get out of it by your own free will, I will drag you out of it.

No. Don't you dare! Don't . . . you . . . dare! She stood back and regarded herself as she shouted, snapped these words at him. What was the use, she thought, to understand the meaning of the box, if you allowed yourself to be made its victim? Or, even worse, if you used it to . . . enclose others in? As she struggled with him to stay in the glass box, she knew what she was really doing.

She was forcing him into it too.

It was what she'd wanted, wanted all along, she saw. They would be in it together. The thought filled her with intense pleasure, and added to that, was her delight in her own cleverness. He had been clever enough to solve the opening of the box, but she had found a way to make him wear a glass box too. And, besides, she had outwitted her witch mother, who had never dreamed, Orysia was sure of that, that it would be possible to live in the box with someone else . . . with Chassa, for no one else really existed, let alone mattered.

How odd it was, she thought, he had wanted to set her free, and he almost had. But . . . she had shut him up in the glass box, instead.

He was sitting glumly.

She knew that now was the time to conquer him forever by surrendering to him . . . not everything, perhaps, at once . . . but by surrendering enough of herself, enough of herself so that she couldn't ever retract, even if she did keep back part or even the largest part.

Chassa, she began tenderly.

He paid no attention. His feelings were hurt; and so were his expectations.

Chassa?

Yes?

Chassa, if you really do . . . love me, will you because you do and because you already know how much I . . .how fond I am of you . . be very patient with Orysia and let her stay part of the time in the glass box . . . until . . . she can get used to being outside of it?

He didn't answer her.

But perhaps you don't love me, she said a little frantically.

He said nothing.

She easily guessed why — his feelings were hurt because he had been opposed in his desire to rescue her, once and for all, from the glass box.

Very well, she said, changing her voice. Perhaps you will drive me home at once, and never see me again?

He said nothing, but he weakened a little, she could see, in his sulk.

Do you, she asked softly.

Yes, he said.

She shuddered as he spoke the word, yes. It was what she wanted him to say. But it also bound her, it meant that, eventually, she had to give herself up to him entirely, which really meant no more of a loss, than that, once it happened, she wouldn't be able, then, to refuse him.

She wanted to sacrifice that privilege right away, at that very moment. For she knew, now, that there was only one reason she could offer to herself to justify, if the worst came to the worst, refusing him. She was of course so heartlessly in love with him, she didn't care if her scheme failed.

She said, do you want me to become your mistress, Chassa?

It was a sudden and devastating penetration.

And as she had calculated, it shattered him. He said nothing. She waited a moment.

For I will, you know.

No, Orysia, he told her.

If that's what you want me to be, she continued. He blathered out something about always having wanted to marry her, from the first moment he had set eyes on her.

Are you asking Orysia to marry you, she asked him.

Yes, he said.

I would like to become your wife, Chassa.

He by this time knew how cunning she was with words. He was about to seize the glass box — she gave him both her hands. Do you promise, he asked her, to become my wife?

Yes, Chassa, I promise. If you will put up with the glass box for a little while longer. Until I have told Mother Orly that . . . you want me . . . to . . . not stay in it any more.

14

Everything made Chassa want to marry Orysia as soon as possible, and only one thing deterred him, the fact that Orysia was so blissfully happy now that she had him, as she said, always with her in the glass box. Nothing so much (to my mind) proves the witchcraft of Orysia's mother, as the effect the glass box now had upon her. It seemed to her as if it were a vase, which as long as it remained intact, as long as it was unbroken, could keep the flowers placed in it, not eternally nor even lastingly, but yet unusually, magically fresh.

But I want you to bear my child, Chassa complained to her.

I would like to, she told him.

Was she afraid of marriage? Chassa asked her.

Yes, she admitted.

Oh no, she re-assured him, she wasn't worried about the physical relationship — but rather, she feared the future, and marriage was the future. The now, it was so very perfect.

Or was she unhappy?

No.

Not really.

Still, she told him, she did want to have his baby. She admitted that would be a great happiness.

She made him tell her about his work. He explained how he was engaged in the senior, decision-making, levels of consumer research. But what is that, she asked. He explained to her that with certain products, like coffee, a consistent quality cannot be maintained, because then the consumer grows accustomed to it, then weary, then ceases to buy it. It is like a rose, he explained. You smell it when you first put it to your nose. But if you hold it there very long, your sense of smell becomes accommodated to its fragrance, and you smell it no longer. Thus, what he had to do, was to see that the quality of products was scientifically improved and deteriorated.

You mean, she said, that you sell worse and worse coffee, until no one buys any. Then you improve the quality little by little, and everyone thinks it a good thing?

Yes, said Chassa.

You must get another job, said Orysia.

Why?

Aren't you engaged in something dishonest?

Making certain that people like the products they buy? That's good business. Human satisfaction and a consistent product quality aren't equatable, any other way, he assured her.

Then, said Orysia, perhaps that's the secret of happiness like ours . . . and, she went on, perhaps . . . perhaps. . .

Chassa didn't like the parallel she drew. They — Orysia and himself — were, he said, unique. And you can't, he told her, draw conclusions from the behaviour of the masses.

True, she admitted, but still . . .

15

Much of the bliss of their existence together in the glass box came from their dreams of when it would be abandoned. Orysia liked to hear him make plans for their marriage. She spoke of their children as if they were already nuisances to him — as if she had to protect and cherish him from them. She wondered if perhaps it was children he wanted — not her. They talked of the house they would build, the gardens they would plant . . . even of where they would go on their honeymoon.

And you will teach me to swim, Orysia asked him.

But the glass box, queried Chassa.

Can't you get your mind off the glass box for just one moment, when I am thinking of how I should like you to teach me to swim.

Yes, he said.

You mean, she shifted the subject, what shall we do with it? Perhaps we could sink it at sea, she thought. They would throw flowers on the place where it sank, she decided.

Flowers, he asked.

Do you hate the glass box so much, she asked him. Just when — with you inside it — I'm finding it so warm and comfortable. Well, at any rate, she said, we could still throw flowers on the place where it sank?

But, he told her, I feel so much outside it.

I don't want you inside it, dear, she said to distract him — not when it sinks.

He suggested that if they both wore it on alternate days, he'd see her point and she'd see his.

You? In *my* glass box?

You'd smash it, she said, rounding the first corner.

Suppose I did, he said grumpily.

The glass would cut you, she said — and it was a sign of the hysterical bliss of the state they were in that she burst into tears at the thought of him, cut by the glass of her mother's box.

He tried another tack.

Let me wear it, so that you can see what it is like, to be with someone in a glass box.

I could guess, she said bluntly.

You are inside it with me, always, she said. Don't you know that? But — having insisted so often that this was so, she could hardly resent his hands passing through the glass box, and — since they did so in order to caress her, ever so gently, she didn't.

In fact, the glass box both provoked and, as it were, permitted this sort of caress, which became more and more venturesome.

Yet she felt that these invasions of the glass box were jealously noted by mother the witch.

They frightened her.

Once, several times, frequently she became sick, and wanted to vomit.

16

I thought *it* was the most ugly thing, said Orysia suddenly, out of the clear of the glass box.

What?

It, said Orysia. As if he must know what she meant by *it*, and be shocked by what she said, or that she even mentioned *it*.

What, said Chassa.

It, said Orysia. I can't say it. Don't ask me to say it. I just can't say it.

My hand, said Chassa? He shifted his hand ever so slightly.

Your hand is like a flower, said Orysia.

It is a flower, said Chassa.

Your hand, laughed Orysia. Oh, she exclaimed, the vanity of the brute, the vanity! He thinks his hands are flowers!

No, said Chassa. *It*.

Oh, it, said Orysia off-handedly.

I like your hand to be there, she confided. She felt that the glass box was dissolved and yet not dissolved, to protect them and free them for each other for always.

Ugly, he asked her. That part of the body which is ours but never ours, except when we give it away?

She pondered what he said.

No, she replied. I meant the way in which babies are born.

17

One of the advantages of the box, said Orysia who was at this time always trying to justify not abandoning the box — is that it enables me to see what Mother Orly is doing. There is a certain clairvoyance in the glass box.

It enables me to keep my eye on poor Mother Orly.

Yes, said Chassa, not very much impressed, at the best of times, by the merits of the glass box.

You think so?

I know it, said Orysia. She's spying on us, and I've suspected it for sometime.

And what's more, she has her light delivery out watching us, too.

How could that be, said Chassa.

I've seen it once, twice, three times now . . . said Orysia.

Then isn't it time, said Chassa, to end with the glass box.

The glass box.

Yes.

And do what?

Get married.

I think we shall have to. I think we shall have to do something, Orysia agreed.

Get out of that damned box, said Chassa brusquely.

Orysia whimpered. We'd best keep it for a little while longer. Could you stand Orysia, she said dropping her voice, if you didn't have the glass box anymore, to protect you from her.

It will, she said in a more matter of fact tone, keep us from being surprised.

But the next night the driverless light delivery of the witch mother seemed openly to be following them. Then, as if they were enemy aircraft, it buzzed them, descending upon them where they were parked, and glaring at them with its lights. It was a not very recent model and the lights were so dim that they could see the unattended, the apparently unattended steering wheel.

Orysia, before Chassa could stop her, hurled herself out of his control, and rushing, regardless of the impeding glass box, straight for the driverless truck, tried to dash out its eyes — its headlamps — with stones which, with almost incredible handling of her glass prison, she had managed to collect.

Orysia, Chassa called out after her.

Don't come, she screamed at him.

He tried to reach her — but the soft edge of the road became frost-free under his feet, and he had to scramble through deep mud, gumbo which stuck to him and made progress difficult. He heard a crack of glass.

Don't come near, he heard Orysia shouting out hysterically.

She had struck one headlamp with her stone.

He saw the driverless light delivery backing up with open throttle. He saw Orysia defying it.

He couldn't tell whether she had abandoned the glass box or not.

But then the driverless Ford clashing its gears shifted into low and then into second. It was heading straight for Orysia. She waited until it almost reached her, and then flung herself at it.

Chassa was close enough, that he almost managed to seize her. But not quite. Apparently the driverless truck (or whoever or whatever was controlling it) *intended* only to menace her, for it swung hard over at the same time as she threw herself into its path.

It struck her only a glancing blow.

He heard her moan and a terrific crash of glass. Almost before she fell, he had reached her side, and caught her up. He himself was struck by a flying fragment of glass, or perhaps wounded himself on the broken glass still encircling her.

It's broken forever, she said.

He picked her up. He brushed aside what broken glass fragments he could. As he carried her to his car, he felt his arms wet beneath her, but couldn't tell whether it was his blood or hers. The driverless Ford seemed to be returning. But when it almost reached them, it seemed to change its mind. It swung full circle round, and roared off down the road. In the opposite direction another car was approaching. It stopped opposite them. Two police officers got out.

Hey, what's going on here, Chassa heard a policeman's voice call out.

A spotlight flashed on them.

Get us to the hospital quickly, Chassa murmured.

18

All the bother of extricating themselves from the inquisitions (which of course they were unable to satisfy) of the police, the nuisance of getting stitches in their cut flesh (but fortunately nothing very serious or disfiguring), the difficulty of finding Myrtil, to obtain his consent to their marriage, was as nothing, now that they had been pronounced man and wife.

It was a simple but sufficient ceremony.

After it was over, Orysia insisted that they go at once to Mother Orly, to let her know what they had done.

But why, asked Chassa.

We must tell the witch mother, said Orysia — if only to set her mind at ease. She might accept you.

Set her mind at ease, grumbled Chassa.

We must.

Must?

Yes, we must. You've married Orysia, darling, haven't you. The witch mother is your mother now, isn't she? And whatever she did — you'll have to forgive her, don't you, darling? How can I sleep up tight and close to you, if I know you are hating the poor little witch mother?

She's my mother-in-law, I admit, grumbled Chassa. But . . . I married you, not. . .

You get the witch mother with me, darling.

Chassa tossed back his head, as if trying to shake the whole matter from his mind.

But he still grumbled. I don't see why, he said, we should have to inform her of what she already knows.

But she'll only think she knows. It'll put her mind at rest to let her know that she knows.

Well, Chassa said unwillingly.

Perhaps you are already repenting that you've married Orysia, she said.

How could you say such a thing?

Then shall we get the witch mother business off our chests? It may do us both a good turn. Trust me, darling. She doesn't really hate us.

19

As she got into bed with Chassa on her marriage night, Orysia had to admit that she'd been wrong about going to see the witch mother. How, she said to her disgruntled bridegroom, can you ever forgive me for putting you through all this?

Chassa said nothing.

He was horribly silent. Completely silent. Orysia started to sob.

I didn't think she would *curse* you, she wept.

The witch mother's first words were, I see you have broken the glass box.

I'm married to Chassa, Orysia told her.

The witch mother glared at him.

He's your son, Orysia told her. Aren't you going to kiss your mother, she said to Chassa.

Chassa made a feeble attempt towards kissing where Mother Orly had just been. For the witch shrugged him aside.

He stood still, foolish and wounded.

I see you have broken the glass box, the witch mother shrilled at Orysia.

You are going to get along famously with Chassa, Orysia said.

Chassa held out his arms to the witch mother.

For a half-instant, Mother Orly hesitated, but then, as if irritated by Chassa's beseeching manner, she waved him aside.

I see you have broken the glass box, she said a third time.

It was then that Chassa forgot himself.

I had supposed, he said ironically, that it was you yourself who broke it.

No, it was I who broke it, Orysia tried to insist but the witch mother paid no attention to her.

She spat in Chassa's face.

I curse you, she told Chassa, and I curse your children. You will be happy if you have no children.

Let's get out of here, said Chassa.

Before we all go mad, he said to Orysia.

Don't worry, said the witch, my curse will follow you wherever you go.

Mettre en conte le dream

If dreams are explorations of the round world which surrounds and transcends the flat world of explanation, then any theory about the nature of dreaming is excluded by definition. How many nightmares are the result of Freud's misdirected researches I'd hate to say. Even the statement I've just made is semanticidal paradox. And since to tell a dream is to convert it from a dreamed to a story-teller's experience, I've no choice but to present it to you in fabliau-form, as if it were a conte by Jacques Ferron, or one of Sheila's or Fred Flahiff's or Jack Shadbolt's anecdotes. If you think I'm unaware how difficult that is to do, let me remind you that my Ph.D. thesis was about Sterne's *Tristram Shandy* and the anecdotal tradition, reaching from Plutarch via Bacon and Shakespeare down to Aubrey's *Brief Lives*. I know one cannot experience another person's dreams; and I admit I am the last person who ought to be encouraged to tell his dreams.

I dreamed this particular dream on the night of September 30th, that is on early Saturday morning, October 1st, 1988. On Tuesday or Monday of this week, Sheila called me, about 10.00 p.m., to see a full or nearly full moon rising over Georgia Straits. The sky was very clear, and the lagoon as flat as glass. Reflected in the lagoon was a second moon, as bright as the one hanging above it. For one, two, three nights after that, we saw the same unchanged full moon, and the same reflection in the same mirror of plate-glass water. The lagoon is an unparalleled master of graphic design, framed by the spit, the south rock, the hump lying east and west, and the north rock, but because of its tidal nature, being sometimes full of seawater, and sometimes dry sea-bed, it is never or rarely guilty of repeating itself. We look out over the lagoon at a sea, the Straits of Georgia, which even with its covering of blue sky or cloud or shelves of fog or marine traffic, jibbing or tacking yachts, fishing boats, tugs with sawdust barges, tugs with rafts of logs, friendly American battleships or less charismatic nuclear submarines, is, from day to day, pretty much the same. The lagoon never is. It never paints two canvases the same. But this week it did, in cahoots with les détroits de Georgia. Perhaps it had achieved absolute beauty of design. I wanted to ask my friend Jorge this question, and have him fly out here to put him on the spot, and see what Sheila and I had seen. I didn't absolutely decide not to ask Jorge my question, but I did toy with asking another, related but less difficult question, what rule of design, since he was a graphic designer, could be drawn from a moon-reflection in the lagoon's tidal mirror and its generating body in the sky, with respect to scale and symmetry? By Saturday night, this question had become irrelevant. Earlier, we had gone out for a brief walk on the spit, and as we approached the half-way mark, we began to hear music. I heard it first, and at first I wasn't sure whether I was hearing it or just imagining I was. As we came to the south rock at the end of the spit the music we were hearing became distinct enough to be recognized as bag-pipe music. Look, said Sheila, and pointed to a dark figure in the shadow of the oak trees on the shoulders of the rock above us. Of course, I said. The drone of his pipes made his figure seem more ghostly than human. Isn't this Piper's Lagoon, I said, and isn't it named after the ghostly piper who always comes to warn of threatening dangers to those living on the lagoon? We crept around the base of the south Rock, and put it between us and the lagoon. The piper's primitive counterpoint of pedal point and melody followed us, drifting above us. Across Georgia Straits, we could see the Nanaimo ferry pushing past the Snake Island light down the low coast-line of Gabriola Island. Credit it with arriving on schedule at the Departure Bay dock at seven-thirty-five p.m., and the time was about seven o'clock. We smoked a cigarette on a log a few feet from the sea's edge, and listened to the piper's tentative mourning. It was dark when we got home. When we looked for a double moon to rise for Jorge Frascara, the lagoon refused the request. What did rise instead was an almost perfect half-moon. We could guess why. It wasn't because the tide had run out, it must have been because the wind had ruffled the reflecting surface of the lagoon's mirror of water. What was mysterious was, why had this half-moon followed so quickly and so precisely after the double full moons we had been observing?

It must have been quite late on the morning of October 1st that I dreamed this particular dream, because when I woke up, it was just before dawn. I dreamed I had gone out scootering with Tsade in the northern wilderness. Jorge was going to make us a roaring fire, to revive us when we got back, and Sheila was going to bake him an upside-down pineapple cake. The scooter has always been my favorite means of travelling. The two scooters I had preserved from my boyhood were of a very primitive, but nevertheless very effective kind. They consisted of a flat board, with a steering wheel at one end, and a fixed wheel at the other end. To operate them, you grasped the handle-bars with both hands, set one foot on the foot-board, and kicked away with the other foot. Scherazade had never operated a scooter before, so I assigned the older slower scooter to her, partly to offset her youthful impetuousness, partly to give my experience and age some authority with respect to hazards never absent from this kind of scootering. But she picked up the essentials of the scooter very quickly and was soon racing ahead of me, and my faster scooter. We were quite a strange pair, she a shameless feminist, and I an elderly, shamefaced male-chauvinist! It was mad of me to think I could compete with her. The *oneiros*-terrain into which we were entering, the northern wilderness, soon put this rivalry aside. Scootering is like kayaking, it focuses one's attention on the compulsive nearness of the world through which one is traveling. We forgot the mechanics of our scooters in our perception of the immaculate loneliness of the northern wilderness: its face like the face of god composed in a peace so absolute it was frightening. For Robin Matthews, his countrymen, that's us, go to the wilderness to kneel down before and become one with its mysterium tremens, the source of their identity, the centre of their preternatural being. Truth is of God, and passes human wit, Yeats said or almost said. I thought of this, my favourite of all misquotations, as we stood there beside our scooters.

It was at this moment, this utterly lonely moment of truth, that we saw our first wolf. Tsade saw it first. Look, she said, or rather cried out in a stage whisper. It has a bird in its mouth, she said. I looked and saw it was followed by another wolf. It has another wolf with it, I said. It was smiling. It's smiling at us, I said. I don't think it's smiling at us, Tsade said. No, I whispered back, I don't think it's seen us. Canines don't have remarkable eyes, Tsade informed me. I know dogs don't, I whispered back. It's the female wolf that has the bird in its mouth, Tsade smiled at me. Poor bird, I said, turning my eyes back from the faintly smiling Tsade to the two wolves and their prey, and my scooter around in the direction of our retreat. I feel like a voyeur, I said. Aren't they small, Tsade said. That's because the wilderness-keyhole through which we are looking at them is so vast, I reasoned. Our senses are not rational; they dream up our experiences, don't they now, I said. Strict measure, I pontificated with my hands on my chin and my elbows on the handle-bars of my scooter, has nothing to do with what we see, hear, taste, smell or touch, has it now? This is why Freud is so wrong. He tries to rationalize our dreams, so that he can cry out against the mind's arithmetic, which is the only thing we have which really counts in our struggle against the totalitarianism of despair expressed so sublimely by Shakespeare: we are such stuff as dreams are made on, etcetera. But dreams count, don't they, countered Tsade, resorting to a Derridan pun. Not really, not for Freud they don't, since he has left himself nothing to count with, I contradicted her, raising my head from my hands and my elbows from my machine, and smiling at her like the female wolf a few scooters' lengths away from us, with the bird in its mouth. Sssh, Tsade whispered, crouching down over her vehicle. I crouched over mine. But the warning came too late. It was then that the wolves saw us. It was the she-wolf who saw us first. What she saw of us startled her. She dropped the bird in her mouth. She snouted our scent with a quick nose. She looked round at the youngling at her dugs, to see if it was paying attention. It was. She repeated her instructions with the conscious gesture of a dancing master with an apprentice in tow. What she said to her pupil could be summed up in a single word, the adverb, *now*. We could read it, too.

Let's go, said Tsade. Yes, let's go, I said almost simultaneously. Where to, she asked. When I hesitated, she took the lead, and tore round and past me with a magnificent kick-start which took her from where she was to where she wasn't. Across that water there, to that bluff, she yelled at me. I tore after her in the direction she had chosen. In a moment we were safe, but only for a moment. At the very instant, having caught our breath, we searched for an escape route, we had our second wolf-sighting. On our left flank, we saw three wolves. All three were smiling, and all three were smiling at us. It almost seemed as if they were acting in concert with the two wolves of our first sighting. We must be in wolf valley, Tsade said. We'll have to climb up out of it. She led the only way we could see of possible escape from the unpleasant dinner engagement the wolves seemed to have in mind for us. Yet for all the danger we were in, I could see she relished the fact that we had exchanged roles; she had become the protector of a male who would have insisted on, as a member of the dominant sex, being her protector. This temporary postponement of disaster didn't mean we were out of danger. All we could do was catch our breath without any time to discuss together strategies of escape. Almost immediately, came our third wolf sighting, and then a fourth, and then a fifth; the third of four wolves, the fourth of five wolves, and the fifth, of from five to seven wolves. We seemed doomed, surrounded. I will stay here and talk sense to them, Tsade said to me. Why? I asked. There's no time for argument, she said. I'm a lot younger than you and more tasty, and they will let you escape while they are relishing me. So get going. I made no move to move. You simply don't know your predators, I told her. All predators, except man, practice their predation on the weak, sick, accident-prone members of the species they feed on. So I will talk sense to our friends; they will accept me as normal food; and you must get away. I didn't think my argument would work, but it left her suggestion exposed as unacceptable. If we were going to have to talk sense to the wolves, we would do it together.

I admit I was, at this point, at my wit's end. As I recall things recollectively, I don't think Tsade was. Sometimes I thought I matched her in intellectual *arete*. But if I did, and I'm not sure that I did even in the realm of *theoria*, in the realm of *praxis* she wore her *arete* with a woman's confidence in the seagull-like adequacy of her avoirdupois, falling, rising, poised. Her bone was not as heavy as a male's, but she made much more skilful use of its weight. It was a beautiful thing to behold, when these, her *arete* and her woman's inwit, her consciousness of being of the superior sex, failed her. At this moment, the climax of my dream, she wasn't angry, but pleased with herself. I don't think she was quite at her wit's end. I think she may have suspected that I was. Thus: she looked at her watch — I too consulted mine, but only to keep attention focussed on the same ideas she had with respect to our predicament, so that we could act out our fate in unison, or at least with or in contrapuntal harmony. What I think she had in mind, was to set up a time-clock of how many minutes or rather seconds we had left together before fate wolfed us down. I took heart from her not being in an obviously prayerful mood. When it came to that, I knew what her prayer, and through her, what mine would be: oh, oh, oh, O sweet dear god, the country, yes, so beautiful it almost converts me back to theocentrism — as an honest-to-god atheist, help me to outwit it, and its magnificent she-wolves and their handsome yuppy-puppy males, and you! It should be obvious to the Freudian investigators of this dream, or rather the story based upon it, that I am not an honest-to-god anything. I admit I was embarrassed at being confronted by a *deus absconditus* who said to me something like the following (while Tsade stood beside me seeming dumb-founded): I am not the three persons of Christian theology. I am not the mechanical accident of scientific speculation. I am not a vast but dissipating energy. I am not the arbitrary culpability of things. Neither am I the beautiful landspaces of Norman Yates. I am not the sun, moon, or star-spangled banner of outer space explorations. I am not the black hole of Nietzsche nor the differences with a difference of the Saussurean Jacques Derrida's in-the-beginning-was-the-word. I am the metaphysical ferment of mean-ings out of which languages grow. Do you understand me, the apparition of the *deus absconditus* asked me. Yes, I replied, no, I said,

I am beginning to misunderstand you, I'm afraid. The face of the apparition had no resemblance to the face on the shroud of Turin. The face I was looking at was rather like that of a stage actor than that of a TV screen. It darkened itself. Have no fear — don't think you have to fall down and worship. You will come to no harm. I have chosen to save you from the jaws of the wolves, said the apparition. I want you to explain me to your people. But am I the best choice, I asked. Wouldn't someone like Margaret Atwood reach a wider audience, I asked. I've thought of her, the apparition said. She's strong on self-promotion, it said. This prevents her from seeing things the way I do. She's not what I had in mind, to do the sort of thing I have in mind. The apparition turned as if about to make an exit. Look, said Tsade, the wolves are almost on us. It doesn't matter whether they eat you or not, said the apparition, exiting. But they won't, the apparition called back, turning, and was gone.[1] At this point, we threw our arms in the air, as if we were skaters in a hockey game which had gone into overtime and our goal had broken the tie with a sudden death decision giving us both the game and the series. We are saved, I cried. It didn't seem to matter much to the surrounding wolves. God, said Tsade, helps those who help themselves. I could see she was trembling. The wolves were almost about to pounce. We are saved, I said. What did you see, I asked her. I don't know what I saw, she said. God, she repeated, helps those who help themselves. She smiled. I saw, she said, I don't know what I saw. What did you see? I saw an Egyptian god with the head of a bird, she jested. What did you see, she asked back at me. I don't know what I

---

[1] I realize that this part of my dream will pose enormous difficulties for some of my readers, especially for those who are agnostics, not atheists like David Hume, the enlightenment philosopher more celebrated in his own day for his atheism than for his rejection of Cartesian mechanism. If he didn't accept mechanical causation, how could he accept a clock-maker god? The atheism of David Hume doesn't surprise me so much as his misunderstanding of Rousseau's alienation. When he was at the point of death, David Hume was visited by James Boswell, who wanted to find out if the dying atheist had repented and changed his mind. Boswell was a stupendous clever fool, but his folly is, like Rousseau's paranoia, more forgivable than Hume's sanity. We do not know what Hume experienced in the last minutes of his crucifixion by cancer. He could only share these with Boswell (and his public) in a fiction as insecure as what I am now attempting.

saw, I replied. I saw a Japanese goddess, with the face of Rose of Lima. Santa Rosa de Lima, Tsade said to me in a quick burst of verbal machine-gun fire, is Fred Flahiff's saint, the saint you don't dare to invoke lest she overwhelm you with assistance. We must go, she added. What did you see, I persisted. I wanted to be very sure what I'd seen, I told her. I remember what I heard, Tsade said. I don't remember what I saw. I saw so many gods and goddesses I don't recall whether they were Inuit or Chinese or Aztec or Greek or Himalayan or Hittite or Haitian or Celtic or — I don't remember, I'm not sure — but — no, we must go. Nevertheless we must, I said, agree on what we saw, otherwise how can we be sure we are saved? We must go, she said. We can at least agree they all had the crucified face of the archetypal mother, can't we, I insisted. I don't remember, she said — perhaps not wanting me to know what she remembered. Do you remember what you saw, she asked me. No, I'm trying to, I said. I remember clearly that I saw something, but not precisely what it was I saw. I remember precisely, she admitted, one of the faces — it was a beautiful male face, like Jorge's. She readied her scooter. The wolves had sent an avant-garde to block our retreat. She pointed her machine directly at them. They reacted with the fierce caution of an armed riot squad picking up unarmed protesters. What's the good, I asked, of being saved, if we don't remember not only what we were saved from but who saved us? What's the good, she said, of remembering anything, if we're not saved and are eaten alive? With a frantic kick of her left foot, she and her machine were off. I was as startled by this Amazonian kick-off, as the wolves. I followed her, as if I was a child being dragged from in front of a car by a frantic mother. Being saved didn't matter to me any more. A new despair possessed me, that when the dream vanishes — and I knew now I was dreaming — and we try to dream it again, we never arrive at the dream we want to recall, it is another dream we arrive at, and from that, another, until we have to be satisfied with the insecure fiction of a series of fictions. But I followed her. She had blasted a way through the party of wolves. They let me pass unmolested. They were no longer a police riot squad. They smiled at me, as if they were glad we had got away from them, confident that they would eventually get us; they were hunters, good sports, glad of a quarry who challenged the odds so heavily in favour of their supper later on, after a gratifyingly hard-earned chase. I didn't acknowledge their sportsmanship as I hurtled past them, to skid to a stop on a ledge Tsade had reached, at reckless speed, moments ahead of me. We stepped off our scooters and let them complete the hockey-players' game-hug of unexpected victory. They fell around each other, as if inedible though they were, they shared our danger of being devoured by the wolves. We leaned back against the Yatesian cliffs they had brought us to, said nothing, stared at each other. You won't believe this, she said to me. I always wanted to have a genuine mystical experience, she confessed. In my wildest dreams, she said, picking her way like a young doe carrying its first fawn, very near term, across a stretch of sea beach, at low tide, with elegance, caution, precision, counterpointing breath and footing — in my most wild dreams, she said, I never hoped, expected or dreamed of anything like this. I imagined a mystical experience to be like that of Bernini's Teresa or Yeats' Leda, swooning backwards in ecstasy or ravished by an unspeakably divine sadism, one-to-one, the feather-duster topping the table-top. I never foresaw being equated to every god and goddess the human mind is or has been haunted by, in so brief a *nunc stans*. Derrida, she began, and stopped short. Yes, I prompted, what about Derrida, I prodded. Derrida's polytheistic-atheism, she said, unravels both god and man. And woman, I said. I would have gone on asking about Derrida. We both of us sensed we were still in the suburbs of a *nunc stans*, a standing now, which we had entered, not like the medieval monk, via the singing of a nightingale, but via the smiling teeth of the wolves. We had reversed roles, not as procreationists, hipsters of an angel-headed chemical bondage, but as voyeurs of the round world, which the cartographers of the flat world can never know, yet know as its *summum bonum*: what ordinary folk call truth. I wanted to articulate, her role. She wanted to riddle out the paradoxes, my role. I felt the ledge against which we leaned grow heavy. I turned my eyes to the narrow horizon at the foot of our ledge. Above, the sky was a bowl of milky light.

Look, I said. It was then that we had our first sighting of bears. There were two of them, a fairly young mother and its year-old daughter. They bounced along like women tourists, having a good time with each other, amused at their own truculence, aware that they were being cheated by the natives, safe in their magnificent fur coats, bumping into everything in their way, jolly about their melancholy weight. Bears never seem to belong, they always seem like foreigners. Almost simultaneously came our second sighting, and then our third. They didn't see us. They saw the wolves, and they also saw that the wolves were having some sort of do, party, celebration. The wolves made it plain they weren't invited. Very well, they would come as uninvited guests. The wolves didn't like this at all, in fact, had been observing preliminary courtesies, before proceeding ceremoniously, they were not gentlefolk, but neither were they gluttons, to the banquet. What the partying wolves tried to do, was to head the uninvited guests the bears off from our presence. It was then that the bears caught sight of us. Lions roar. Wolves howl. Eagles scream, cougars and human babies. Bears utter a deep rumbling basso-profundo grumble, as if grumbling and laughing an ill-natured laughter at having to grumble. As uninvited guests often are, they were in a good humour, these bears almost upon us. They didn't bellow in unison, but all at once and everyone separately. It hit my ears like a shipload of aggressive tourists: this ursine resentment of inhospitality, a laughing it off, yes — yet still very close to tears and human misery. The wolves moved round their uninvited guests and threw around them an entanglement of howling with skilful ventriloquism. What now seems comic in the fictional space of a *conte* in the real space of my dream seemed catastrophic. What possible remission could there be now, to the peril we faced? The wolves were minueting around the bears. The bears were dancing a *la volta* around the wolves. It was startling to behold the heights to which they could leap up such masses of bone, muscle and fur. But at any moment one of these beasts might decide to break ranks and turn attention to us, and we would be lost. Our only escape route was up the cliff behind us. We would have to drag each other up it. Our faithful scooters had carried us to where we were. Now we would have to drag them after us. Tsade read my thoughts. What about them, she asked me. We'll need them later on, I told her. Later on, she asked. Her voice was matter-of-fact. The passionate fear which had energised her *arete* had left her. I let my eyes scan her face. It was like the face of the moon when it seems to be listening to a private music. I shut my eyes, using my eyelids to exclude the message I didn't want: peace. God, I said, repeating her earlier injunction, helps those who help themselves. Then I seized her and dragged her, notch by notch, to the level above us. When that was reached, I repeated the procedure. As soon as the process was underway, Tsade seemed to reverse herself, and follow my lead. When I was exhausted with dragging her up the cliff-face, she would drag me. Using both our strengths alternately, we reached safety. I had to go back for first one scooter, then the other. Down below, the party of the wolves and the bears had become noisy and violent.

When I reached the summit with the scooters, there were three things to be done, preparatory to our safe return. First, to oil our machines, next to divide up our emergency rations; and finally, to consult our maps. Each scooter had its own saddle-bag, attached, since the scooter doesn't have a saddle, to the steering-post. When we checked, we found two sets of emergency rations, one set (incomplete) of maps, and one oil-can. It had plenty of oil, but was leaky, and had ruined the maps, and one set of rations. I oiled the machines while Tsade divvied up the rations. We ate what was edible of the spoiled rations. She said nothing about the spoiled maps. I went through them looking to see if I could salvage some help from them, but each time I did so they seemed to have deteriorated further. What will we do without them, Tsade asked. Rely on our sense of direction, I said. You think it was the bears who saved us, Tsade said. Yes, I said. No, she said. It was the bears who saved us from the wolves; but it was the wolves who saved us from the bears. What about that squirrel, I asked her. There had been a lone squirrel there with a voice like a treble dissecting knife. The squirrel, she wondered. I wondered what trespass had justified its auricular corkscrew.

The return home began uneventfully. The world beneath us stretched out like a map. It was well supplied with rivers to follow. Which one should we choose, Tsade asked. You are good at choosing, I said. The obvious one to choose, she decided, is that one. It fell in leisurely harmonic curves to the south and west. So we chose it. As a choice, it was a good choice. To use the land one travels through as a map, however, is not without difficulties. The secret of not getting lost, is to realize that as you travel forward the map changes; and you can't turn back to previous charts you've been using, to make corrections. Our scooters helped us. They had no qualms about the way we were going, but moved with a new energy, almost like horses on the return home.

They pulled us very fast down the harmonic curves of the river Tsade had chosen. Yet we seemed to be parachuting down in long slow cadences, suspended almost without motion. Every moment suggested syntactical links with the flat world of common, non-dreaming existence, the world we wake up into. In a tone-poem, the notes of a horn may suggest a forest scene. Some of these tonal similes were very fantastic: the *conte* ought to make some gesture toward them however powerless to accurately translate them. Thus: the scooters suggested the animal-machines of Descartes, the Rational Horses or Houynhnhmns of Swift, the human machines with an animal mind of twentieth-century psychiatry. From the mechanical cats of Descartes, able to feel no pain, yet able to mime it with exquisite accuracy, I went on to think of Descartes in a Quebec logger's jersey and boots, cutting down all the trees in the world he could, with his *dubito* as a double-bittered axe, to prove that the axe was real. At this point in my dream, in the exchanges of waking and sleeping, I thought of Reid MacCallum, who taught me the rudiments of Descartes' philosophy. What Descartes dreamed of, MacCallum said, was a mechanical world which could be treated mathematically. It was at this point my career began, but it took a sudden comic turn, and a new look at Descartes through the eyes of Lawrence Sterne's *Tristram Shandy*. Tristram's autobiography is really Sterne's, ghosted by a running-down machine. Through an accident, Tristram at his conception is stamped with the image of a running-down clock. His account of his life strikes a deadly satiric blow at the weakest point of mechanism, its failure to see that machines break down, need repairing, wear out, disintegrate. Tristram romanticises his physical break-down. Similarly, developing science romanticised its growing awareness of the fatal flaw in mechanization. Today, the tendency of the machine to self-destruct, which Sterne points to, has become a destructive force threatening the entire globe with extinction. — These were some of the thoughts that flashed through my dreaming mind as our faithful scooters carried us down one turn of the river after another on our way back home, or to some point where we could expect to be rescued from.

From time to time Tsade looked back over her shoulder to see if I was keeping up with her, and I would wave at her and she at me. Why my thoughts had become so gloomy, between these interpersonal exchanges, I don't know. Partly it was, I suppose, because I had furnished my mind with ideas from the books of writers who, though cheerful men, were unable to write about the world of today with much cheerfulness: Illych, Lifton, Ellul, McLuhan. Partly it was because of the fear in my heart that the beautiful river-scape we were passing through was being readied for Descartes' chain saw. We entered a wide river plain. Our scooters powered by gravity had carried us here as if they enjoyed their task. Now we would have to propel them. Tsade waved back to me suggesting a halt. I had no option but to agree, for at that moment my scooter collapsed under me. I was thrown into a thicket of grass, unhurt. My machine had completely disintegrated, as if it had exploded. I struggled to my feet only to see Tsade, a few car lengths ahead of me, flying through the air. Almost simultaneously with mine, her machine had exploded under her, disintegrated. The lush grass which had rescued me, broke her fall. It was as if our devoted servants the scooters, unable to serve us any longer, had decided to render up the ghost together. All that we could salvage from the double accident, were the two saddle-bags, containing one ration of food and a set of useless maps. I ran to Tsade with my saddle-bag, and she ran towards me with hers. You must be

Dr. Livingstone, she said. And you must be Mr. Stanley's sister, I replied. A beautiful place to be rescued from, she said. Yes, I agreed. I wonder what caused it, she said. The accident, I asked. She seemed to be accusing herself of having provoked it, by calling for a halt. Perhaps they chose this tuft of grass, as a soft spot to deposit us in, I said. Or the grass itself may have reached out to make our acquaintance. I admit I have a frivolous imagination. The word wonder, used at the scene of an accident, induces it to hallucinate. Perhaps, I said, the cause of the accident was the result of a conspiracy between our servants the scooters and their friends and our friends, the grasses, reeds, rushes, vetches, mosses. Every accident has its causes, I said, except one. Which one is that, Tsade asked me. The primal one of scientific belief, I said. And even that one leads most of us to wonder, what caused it. Like me, Tsade thought of our scooters more as friends than as mechanical servants. I don't like to leave them here, she said, without giving them a decent burial. I looked to where their ashes had fallen. Already the long grass was closing over them. I raised my eyes up, and thought I saw a speck, a disturbance, in the sky. It's a helicopter, Tsade assured me. We're rescued, she shouted. We're not only saved, I said, we are rescued. It hardly occurred to us that, since its crew wasn't looking for us, we mightn't be seen. We danced a 'here-we-go-round-the-maypole' dance of may-day supplication. But we soon saw that they had spotted us. Very cautiously they approached us, as if fearful of an ambush. They criss-crossed then hovered over us. The chop-chop-chop of their rotors became so deafening that we put our hands over our ears and danced with elbows extended as if not wanting to hear the music we were dancing to. I wanted to shout to Tsade, this is ludicrous, but she couldn't have heard me. What was more ludicrous was that, when they had dropped down so close to us that we were almost blown away, they withdrew. It was as if we were being punished for the ingratitude with which we had rejected the vortex of atonality they lived in. But they didn't abandon us completely. They withdrew to a considerable height, and waited, directly over us. Then to our relief, other helicopters arrived. They circled around the waiting ship. I couldn't help wondering if what we had thought of as rescue, was a species of hostile arrest. Then the assembled helicopters dropped to the ground, one by one. Their loud-hailers blasted messages to us, but these were too loud to be heard. We just stood there, waiting. When all had landed, and we were completely encircled, they switched off their engines. If this were a military operation, it was one of extreme tactical clumsiness. Possibly we were too inconsiderable a target, too unspecialized for its enormous power and complexity. If we had had the assistance of our scooters, we could have easily darted past these new high tech molesters, and evaded them, and escaped, as we escaped from the wolves. These technological transvestites hadn't the expertise of the wolves, or even of the bears. These men, if they were men, and not robots, who tumbled out of the gunships, at first seemed like bears, without the majestic furs of these animals, and without the bouncy animal cunning of the bear. They were presumably totally frustrated by their anti-chemical, anti-biological warfare outfits, artificial armour which made it impossible for them to respond naturally to the evils that, if they had not created, had been magnified to infinity by them. An enormous battery of loud-hailers told us we were under arrest for violating their strategic space. Even when we sheltered our ears with our hands, it was impossible to make sense of what instructions were being blasted at us from all directions and in all directions. When they tried to handcuff Tsade she refused to co-operate. So they turned on me. I followed her example. We never heard a human voice. We dodged this way and that, and even began to relish our successful evasions. Our situation was painful, not pleasant, yet it was good to see that human beings could so easily stand off cybernetic monsters. In fact, what we were seeing (and hearing) was the last stage of development of the Cartesian animal-machine. This machine at first seemed to have acquired a human soul. That seemed to give it an utopian usefulness. But as the machine developed in complexity, so the psychical centre which controlled it, its transplanted cybernetic mind, reversed into a fiendish, suicidal, propensity. We heard the loud-hailers blaring out, don't bother with them. And the robot crewsmen returned to their ships. These then started to lay a carpet of poison enough to take care of a battalion. To rid themselves of two ants, they would render an entire mountain range untenable, who knows for how long? When I saw we couldn't evade their unnatural excretions, I contracted every muscle in my body, let go of my dreaming body, and woke myself up.

It was the morning of October 1.

The Baie-Comeau Angel

After the elections of 1984, John Turner, who was badly defeated, in utter despair asked for a consultation with the devil. This he arranged through his psychiatrist, a Toronto witch with a very select and successful practice. What can I do for you, the Evil One asked. John Turner told him. The Evil One shook his head understandingly enough. Yes, Turner said, I want to kill myself. Why, asked the Evil One. Because, Turner said, from now on no one who isn't a French-Canadian can ever become Prime Minister of Canada. I thought, the Evil One said, Prime Minister Mulroney was an Irishman? He certainly sings like an Irishman, said Turner, but he speaks faultless French. It's that that defeated me. The Evil One laid his hand on John Turner's shoulder. Don't use your gun on yourself, he said. Use it on Mulroney. I can't do that, John Turner said. If you loved your country enough, you could, said the Evil One. It's the only way you'll beat Mulroney. Turner shook his head. The Evil One ended the consultation. John Turner put his gun away. For the moment, the horror of the devil's proposal purged him of his suicidal despair. He went to bed and slept peacefully. The next day, he woke up almost a happy man, but when he went to select a shirt-stud, from his stud-box, his fingers fell among the bullets he had removed from his army pistol after his consultation with the devil. One of these bullets was of Peruvian silver, a family heirloom. His despair returned with irresistable intensity. He replaced the bullets in his pistol, raised the muzzle to his brow, and was about to press the trigger, when the devil stopped him, appearing uninvited. I love Canada too, said the Evil One. So I will help you. And he whisked John Turner into Mulroney's office. The Prime Minister was seated at his desk alone, with a bottle of Ontario wine, a gift from the blue machine, and trying to select a cabinet from a heap of photographs. Now, said the devil. John Turner pulled the trigger, and shot the Prime Minister dead. He would have used the Peruvian silver bullet on himself, but quick as a shot is, the Evil One was quicker. He seized John Turner and whisked him back to where he was, and deposited him on a large, comfortable chesterfield embroidered with apple-blossom and roses. Then the devil departed, first removing the army pistol which was still in Turner's hand, wiping it on his silken turtleneck, and setting the safety catch. But a Baie-Comeau angel, a very simple one, rushed to the scene of the crime, a crime so horrible that, simple as he was, he was at a loss as to what he must do. So he knelt down trembling beside the dead body and prayed to the Blessed Virgin Mary to help him. When, said the Blessed Virgin Mary, I bake a cake, and it burns, I bake another one. Folks forget, she added, I am not only a virgin, but a wife, and a mother, a housekeeper, and a cook. A cook, repeated the angel, a cook? He had expected that the Blessed Virgin would intercede with her Son to raise the Prime Minister from the dead. Inspired by the Blessed Virgin's words, the Baie-Comeau angel set about to act creatively. This is what she wanted of him, not another Lazarus, by her intercession, but a brand-new Mulroney, in the creation of whom he would have a humble part: not a spoiled loaf of bread, but a freshly baked one. Thus it was that the most ineffectual of angels, this Baie-Comeau angel who had never even boiled an egg, or a potato in its jacket, with all the creative resources of heaven at his disposal, replaced the dead Mulroney with an almost perfect replica of the live one. The real Mulroney was never missed. How the Baie-Comeau angel handled the security guards will probably never be known for certain. There was a corpse. This had to be disposed of. There was a photograph with a bullet hole in it. This had to be taken care of: the photograph the assassinated man had held up to protect himself from the assassin's gun. Almost certainly, the Baie-Comeau angel dealt with these problems, if not instantaneously, almost instantaneously, before substituting the new Mulroney for the old one. He loved the old one very dearly. It wasn't to be just discarded like a growing reptile's snakeskin. It would be ridiculous to suppose that the Baie-Comeau angel, as soon as he had dealt creatively, simple as his intelligence was, with the awful fact of the assassination, shared the human artist's preference for the work of art over its object, like Picasso's preference for the painting over the women he painted. All my paintings are fakes, Picasso told his admirers. The Baie-Comeau angel might not have thought of the new Mulroney as a fake. He probably thought of him as nearly perfect Xerox, to be intuited as preferable in most respects to the worked-over original. Without the slightest vanity, but with justification, he preferred his copy for the beauty of its cleanness to the author's foul papers. It took the new, substituted Mulroney only a few minutes to adjust to his role, and recall what he was doing, selecting a cabinet.

When John Turner regained full consciousness, he staggered up from the apple-blossom and roses embroidery of the couch on which the devil had bestowed him, and called Tilly-the-know-it-all his secretary to find out about the crisis he was sure had happened. He knew he must betray no knowledge of it. There's no news at all, she told him, except the weather. It's really dirty. I wasn't expecting to hear any bad news, he said. But hoped something had gone right for once. I don't know, I don't know, she said. She spoke to him in French, he spoke to her in French. Your French is improving, she said. But I don't know of anything else that is, she said, there may be, there may be, but I don't know of it. He decided to let the news come to him. He looked for his pistol. He knew he hadn't left it at the scene of the crime. He did remember clutching it, before he passed out on the couch where the devil had plunked him down. He thought of praying. He tried to say his prayers. But the words wouldn't come. Even the words his mother had taught him: Please God make me a good boy, and Gentle Jesus, meek and mild, look upon a little child, wouldn't come. The thought that he was damned gave him a sort of cold inner peace. He recalled how he had once explained to a group of students from the Harvard School of Business that the rules of morality are what one must do, and that the rules of ethics pertain only to what one mustn't do, like not putting sand in the sugar, or water in the treacle; and like loving and caring. There was a trap in these words. Quick as a shot, a bright young student had sprung it on him. Sir, he said, aren't you asking us to choose between Christian morality and Jewish ethics? The devil had caught him with the same trap: the choice between 'thou shalt not kill' and loving your country with all your heart and soul. He couldn't help but admire the young business school radical's bright handsome face. If he hadn't admired the devil's cunning, why had he sought out a consultation with him? The blessed thing about knowing one is damned, is nothing else matters any more. You just don't give a damn. Truth is irrelevant. As morning approached and he waited for the news that didn't come, he gave himself up to this lie: I have acted purely out of love of my country. After their long years in opposition, the Tories had perfected an art of political lying. This they had brought up-to-date, modernized. They had revitalized it with help from the private sector. The term itself is a semantic deception for big, small, medium-sized business. During his Bay Street years he had grown to hate it with a post-fundamentalist ardour, like that of Ivan Illych, the medical dissenter, or like that of Jacques Ellul, who demonstrated, as if it was a theorem in mathematics, why high technology had to become the evil angel of government-supported defense industry. The lies of the media, public relations campaigns, advertising he saw as worse than murder, whether self-destruction, or the wiping out of another. The finger that pressed the trigger which killed Mulroney had been the devil's finger. So here he was lying to himself about his noble damnation. So he waited. But no news came.

No photo-event greeted him when he reached the House. There was an absolute absence of crisis. As he went towards his seat, he saw that Brian Mulroney was already in the House ahead of him. Or seemed to be. They would have exchanged glances, across the floor of the House, which was only spottily attended; but he dropped his eyes down and aside. Fearfully he recalled his *Macbeth*: Mulroney seemed to be staring at him. Not accusingly, not reproachfully. But poised between reproach and accusation. He sat with his head down. He even disregarded a call from the Speaker. He tried to think himself into the state of cold self-appraisal he had enjoyed earlier the evening before.

When he had pulled the trigger and shot Mulroney dead, a decision
had been acted upon that excluded all other decisions. This ultimate
decision had been a snap-judgment, an unpremeditated reversal of a
long meditated intention, to do away with himself. It was a leap in
the dark which involved a leap into absolute darkness. But once the
jump had been made, it had clarified mind (and soul) for him. Now
that almost blessed state of clarity had been snatched away from
him. Mulroney had triumphed, once again. Mulroney had reduced
him to the old agony of decision-making. The decisions to be made
were critical. He could leap to his feet and say to the speaker, I rise
on a point of privilege. I have murdered the Prime Minister. His death
will soon be discovered. I have no regrets. Let history judge my
motives. The shape I see before me, and you see, is a ghost. —But how
could he make such a statement. He was in the real House, not
hallucinating in a Shakespeare play. Of course, what he saw might
be an hallucination. Or he might have dreamed he had murdered
Mulroney. The devil might have cheated him. The last possibility
should have brought him decisive relief. But it didn't. There *is*
something blessed about knowing one is damned; something hellish
about being in a state of despair, which, because the negation of hope,
is related to hope, and so has an element of hope; which though not
without remedy, is nevertheless dubiously curable. —He got up, and
left his seat, and fled down the corridors of the House. By the time
he got to his office, he realized that he MUST have dreamed that he
had shot Mulroney dead. The devil MUST have deceived him. The
only way to find out, and be certain, was to consult the Evil One once
again. He would have to telephone his psychiatrist, the Toronto
witch, once again to arrange a consultation. He still (and he smiled
grimly at his credulity as he reflected that he did so) believed in the
Evil One. He couldn't very well telephone his psychiatrist from his
office. So he left the House, and sought a safe, outside, telephone.
The psychiatrist told him several hours later, that the Evil One was
on a fishing trip in Alberta. Does that surprise you? she asked him.
No, he said, Alberta is Tory territory. He has an influential client in
southern Alberta, the witch said. They are fishing together in Lac La

Biche. Lac La Biche, Turner told her, isn't in southern Alberta. Well, that's where they've gone to, the witch said. Turner agreed to a consultation in Edmonton, after the week-end was over. He bit his finger-nails until then. On Tuesday, he found the devil in an excellent frame of mind. The white fish must have been really biting. And what's biting you now, John, the devil greeted him. He wanted to say, and how is Peter these days? — he was sure that the Evil One's 'influential client' was a well-known provincial politician of that name. Instead, he came directly to the point. It was just a dream, wasn't it, he asked the devil. No, said the devil, it wasn't just a dream. It was not the answer Turner expected. You mean I pulled the trigger of a real gun and fired a real bullet into the heart of a real Mulroney? Turner asked. Yes, said the Evil One, smiling condescendingly. You did indeed fire a real bullet into — into the heart of the problem, your problem. And thereby, said Turner, committed murder most foul, as in the best it is? I wouldn't put it in those words, said the Evil One. Then how would you put it? Turner asked. I would say, the Evil One answered, that you committed a political and needful act out of love of your country. Then how come Mulroney is still alive and govern-ing the nation? Turner blurted out. He isn't, said the Evil One. But he is, insisted Turner. I saw and heard him with my own eyes and ears. Only trust half of what you see, the Evil One told him, and nothing of what you hear. And, the devil went on to explain, what you saw, and what the rest of the world sees, isn't the real Brian Mulroney, but a replica. I don't believe it, said John Turner. You'd better believe it, said the devil. Then the real Brian Mulroney is dead? enquired Turner. Yep, said the devil. And buried, asked Turner. I don't know what happened to the remains, said the Evil One. Suitably disposed of, I suppose, he added. I don't understand at all, Turner told him. You will, when I've explained to you what hap-pened, the Evil One assured him, but waited. And how were the fish biting? Turner asked abruptly. I mean, he explained, you were on a fishing trip here — so I was told. Oh yes, said the Evil One, happy as a lark to talk about his prowess with bait and hook. I landed, he said, the biggest fish ever landed in Alberta; and I didn't even have to bait my hook. He baited it himself, with himself. No, scoffed John Turner. What I really meant, he said, was — I don't bite. You won't have to, said the devil. When I catch you, John, it won't be with a hook and bait. I will use a net. You will swim right into my arms. I love you, John. My way with you is the way of a maid with a man, of a man with a maid. If you don't want me, I don't want you. — As for your question, Sunday was an especially good day. What I meant, said John Turner, was that I don't accept your explanation *re* Brian Mulroney as a replica. You haven't heard it, said the Evil One. Wait till you hear it. Listen.

When the devil had outlined to John Turner how the Baie-Comeau angel had interfered with his plans, he offered Turner the choice of breaking off the consultation at that point, or of continuing it. There may be, the devil said, some questions you will want to ask, that I can clear up immediately. Indeed, there were. Yes, I do have some questions to ask, said Turner. I think, he observed, I must be the most conspicuous failure of all time. Don't you agree? No, said the devil. Well, what have I accomplished? Turner asked. I have committed a ghastly crime, with what results? An angel from Baie-Comeau, so you say, replaces the dead Mulroney with a perfect replica. How have I benefitted Canada? I have failed both in action, and in judgment. Surely, said the Evil One, Canada is better off with an imitation Mulroney than with the real one? When no one, said Turner, except you and me, and I suppose, the Baie-Comeau angel, can tell the difference. Plenty of people can perceive the difference, said the devil. They may not be able to explain it. And, he added, however much the Blessed Virgin might have empathised with the Baie-Comeau angel's infatuation for Mulroney, it's hardly likely she would permit him to whomp up an equivalent without some modification, some pious improvements, is it? Then what do you propose I do now? Turner asked. What do you want to do? asked the Evil One. I want to get out of politics, Turner said. And leave the Canada we both love, the devil replied, to the mismanagement of an imposter who if an improvement on the real Mulroney is still an imposter? As I read the perturbation in your heart, John, I don't think that's what you want to do. Then advise me, said Turner. Tell me what I should do. O.K., said the devil. Get rid of the imposter. How am I to do this? Turner asked. In the same way as you disposed of the real Mulroney. Another assassination, asked Turner. Yes, said the Evil One. Good God, no, shouted Turner. Yes, said the devil. But if I could manage to screw up my courage for another shot at Mulroney, Turner began. It won't be another shot at Mulroney, all that's required is a pot-shot at an imitation of him. Surely your country and mine demands us to think clearly about what is required of us. My love of Canada, said Turner, isn't negotiable. Surely everybody knows that. Unfortunately, John, Canadians by and large have a thing about patriotism. They don't believe in love of country. So they're blind to it. But, the Evil One added, I know how strongly you feel about Canada; and so must the Baie-Comeau angel when he finds out that you are prepared to risk what common folks call damnation for your country. Excuse me, said Turner. If I murder the present replica, won't the Baie-Comeau angel produce another replica, and another, and another, until he shames me into turning my gun on myself? Which I should have done in the first place; which I wish I had. The Evil One smiled. They will only be fake murders, he said. Not to me they won't be, said Turner. Nothing will persuade me to turn myself into a multiple murderer, into a Clifford Olsen, nothing. Except a declaration of war? asked the Evil One. Except a declaration of war, Turner repeated, puzzled. Yes, said the devil, a declaration of war. But it may never come to that.

They were sitting in front of a log fire, in a house which had been loaned to the devil by his Alberta client. It was on the north bank of the Saskatchewan River. The afternoon sun was shining through the girders of the High Level bridge. The devil got up from his chair abruptly, as if to indicate that the consultation was over. He walked around the room. John Turner remained slumped in his chair. John, the Evil One said, staring out of the window at the frozen river below, I don't care what you do. As I see my role, it is to help my clients think clearly about the goods they are pursuing. This is how my function is clearly defined in the Book of Job. Have you read the Book of Job?

the evil adviser asked. Yes, of course I have, said John Turner, but not recently. How recently John, the devil asked, but didn't pursue his question. He knew he had positioned her majesty's loyal Leader of the Opposition into not letting the Baie-Comeau angel succeed with his coup. Suppose, said Turner, the Baie-Comeau angel decides not to make another replica Mulroney? It's a possibility, said the devil. Artists usually want to repeat their artistic successes. But though I have had a great deal of experience with human artists, I haven't had any experience at all with the angelic brand. The evil adviser put his arm around John Turner's shoulder. I want to help you, John, the devil said. I'm not a native-born Canadian, but I love Canada as if I were, he explained, and think of it as my own country. The Baie-Comeau angel is also a Canadian of sorts, and mustn't be allowed to put his infatuation for Baie-Comeau above his and my and your love for Canada. The devil gave Turner a brotherly hug. Shall I call you a cab, he asked. Where's home tonight? he asked. He was an expert at applying this sort of personal pressure, warm, physical, considera- tion. I have a flight to Vancouver, Turner told him, but my real home is . . . Bay Street? the Evil One asked, smiling. Oh hell, said Turner, looking down at the frozen river. Well, said the devil, when you get there, load your gun and don't forget the silver bullet, eh? And I will supply all the necessary logistic support.

If we are inclined to cry out in exasperation that this meeting between the devil and John Turner is sheer fairy story, we should remind ourselves of the world of simulated realities in which the media enclose us, which we believe in only because we keep saying to ourselves, over and over again, the medium is the message. But Marshall McLuhan could easily have said, the medium is the mirage; we live in a pure fairy story world. Be that as it may, in the succeeding months, but not at all successful sessions, of the real Prime Minis- ter's 1984 mandate, the little Baie-Comeau angel was called upon not once only, but seven times to supply a replica for the real Prime Minister. Each replica was an improvement on the last, and so each new copy of Mulroney became less and less like the real Mulroney. Who can know for sure, but in all probability the Baie-Comeau angel excused his deception of the Canadian people with an artist's rationalization that the deceit was both innocent and creative. He seems to have been pleased to proceed in a cloud of artistic glory. It was for John Turner quite otherwise. These were the darkest days of his life. Each time he fired his pistol at the next replica was a repetition of the original murder. Each time he acted out the initial assassination required of him a total abandonment of self. He had to screw himself up to an almost unendurable pitch. He suffered the pains of someone who had damned himself over and over again. He wondered if any other person in the whole of history had ever endured the pangs of damnation to the extent he had. When the seventh replica took his place as Prime Minister in the House, Turner's courage broke down completely. Turner knew he couldn't continue. He decided to make a public confession. Rather, he knew he must make a public confession. For months, though his party's rating was high in the polls, the press had been harping on Turner's incompetence and unreliability as a leader. A public confession would expose him as a laughing-stock, and destroy his party's slim chances in an election which was expected in the fall of 1988, or the coming spring. Every day was a torture to him. At night he had repeated nightmares. These were understandable enough; they related to his sense of guilt. His obsessive preoccupation with his damnation did afford him one small mercy: he came to see that simple repentance might be less an ordeal than the virtuous damnation he had resolved upon, out of love of his country. But whenever he resolved to renounce politics (and hence, love of his country) the Baie-Comeau angel's seventh copy would smile at him that deadly unreal smile which was his trade-mark. He realized that it was not in his power not to love Canada.

One night he had quite an unusual dream. It took him back to a holiday he had spent in France, in the French Pyrenees. He had spent several delightful days on the farm of a shepherd who managed to cling on to the old ways of sheep-raising by accepting a few chosen paying guests. He dreamed he was back on this farm. It was lambing time. The good shepherd, his host, was also a stern one. The lambs had been separated from the ewes. The ewes grumbled. The lambs accepted their grassy enclosure as if it was a new freedom, and began to dance. The shepherd looked from them to him, smiling and shaking his head. He turned his dreaming eyes from the shepherd to the dancing lambs. He knew what they were being prepared for. But when the shepherd started to dance a grotesque jig, he took the shepherd's hand, and joined in. This was the end of his dream, but not quite. As he danced away from the fading image of the French shepherd, he was stopped by a woman in archaic dress and with an alabaster face. Stop, she said, what are you dancing for? Because the lambs were dancing, he said. She smiled, then disappeared, and he woke up. He had had the experience and missed the significance of his dream, but it was its significance or significances, which haunted him in the days just before the calling of the 1988 election. He felt an obsessive need to speak out, even if to his own destruction. He was prepared to throw himself away, but there were some things he didn't want to throw away, heedlessly — his party, his friends, his country.

He had a young Jesuit friend whom his associates called Father Vinyl because he spent time collecting and playing recordings of musical Masses, by composers from Guillaume de Machaut to Hindemith. He asked him, in an off-hand way, who is the most political cardinal in Canada. Cardinal Carter is your man, said Father Vinyl. So he made an appointment to see the Cardinal. I warn you, he told the Cardinal, I have to confess an unbelievably horrible crime. The Cardinal looked at him out of eyes of compassion, practiced, churchly, palpably a little bored. Sinners, he chided the would-be penitent Leader of the Opposition, usually attach too much importance to their sins and their confessions. Father, John Turner began, and remembered he had not been briefed (since he had spoken of this meeting with no one) on what to call a Cardinal of the church, and went on, but should I call you father? My child, said Cardinal Carter, call me father, if you wish. Father, Turner continued, I think I must make a public confession. And I am prepared for that. The Cardinal didn't agree. Molière, he said, thought the most beautiful theatre in the world to be two bare boards and a passion. Today people think it is a television screen and a horror story, preferably a horror story with a political slant. I am convinced I must make a public confession, Turner said. It is your final temptation, said the Cardinal. It will turn into an act of self-gratification. You will think it carries with it automatic absolution. Even when the Cardinal had heard every grisly detail of Turner's horror story, he didn't change his advice, but imposed it as an injunction of the church. What you must do to be saved, said the Cardinal, but Turner interrupted him, I don't want to be saved. What you must do to be saved, my child, the Cardinal continued, is go ahead and win the next election for your party, and do so without mentioning anything about your consultation with the Evil One, your assassination of the real Mulroney or the Baie-Comeau angel's substitution of an art nouveau replica. Was this advice, John Turner couldn't help thinking, that of the political Cardinal or of the churchman? For the first time during his meeting with the Cardinal, Turner allowed himself to smile. The Evil One had wanted him to think clearly. The Cardinal wanted obedience. The distinction pleased him. Yet the Cardinal's seeming acceptance of the truth of his horror story made him wonder: wouldn't other people find it acceptable, too? Very well, he said to the Cardinal, absolution depends on my winning the election? I didn't say that, said the Cardinal.

Turner limped out of the Cardinal's presence, disturbed as ever, but not disheartened. The Baie-Comeau angel's alliance *qua* artist with the Blessed Virgin worried him, though not a devout believer, certainly not a post-fundamentalist, like an incurable cancer. What the Cardinal showed him was that the Baie-Comeau angel had his problems, too. These were obvious from the very beginning of the 1988 election campaigns. The Prime Minister swept across the Dominion of Canada as if he were a magician, a master of illusions. One by one, the polls adjusted themselves to the Tory leader's campaign. They seemed indisputable, yet no one believed them. The CBC, fascinated by the world "out there", but institutionally unable to reach out to it, took them on, unsuccessfully. John Turner's

Liberal Party seemed in hopeless disarray. By the time the CBC managed to arrange a debate between the leaders of the three parties, the New Democrats were already counting on forming the next opposition. Every one predicted that the Prime Minister would easily win the debate in French. Most people thought that he would also win the debate in English, though some foresaw a tie between him and Ed Broadbent, the New Democrat leader. What happened was like an earthquake, which shook Canada from shore to shore. How did John Turner, the media asked, manage to defeat, with his imperfect French, Brian Mulroney, with his perfect French? There were many attempts to answer this question, none satisfactory. Yet the answer was perfectly obvious. The Cardinal in his simple wisdom had shrewdly foreseen it; but then he alone had heard John Turner's story about the Baie-Comeau angel. From the very start, the election had become a contest between the unreality of the Prime Minister, and the reality, however compromised, of John Turner.

If the nation had gone to the polls immediately after the CBC debates, the results might well have been a minority government for the Liberals, or at least, only a minority government for the Tories. But election day was still some distance away. What saved the election for Brian Mulroney was not the shouting down of John Turner's veracity with the word, "Liar." This horrified the electorate. It did no harm to Turner, and it revealed the Prime Minister's spurious rhetoric in the ugliest possible light. As the Tory cabinet joined in the outcry, Liar, liar, liar, they seemed to be imitators of their leader's hysterical nullity, deafening, but absolutely unreal. All that Turner had to do was to firmly deplore their abusive language. This he did, with fair success, until he could stand the abuse showered on him no more. Everyone hates to be called a liar. It hurts more than any other term of abuse perhaps because we all know there is some truth in it. The chorus of abuse shouted at John Turner, it will be remembered, came from a group of the most powerful, and most honourable, men in the land, the Prime Minister's cabinet, trained to eschew, and apologise, in Parliament, for using the word *liar*, even when pressed to do so by some exceptionally aggravating deception. To the electorate they seemed more like a pack of fascists, than candidates in a democratic election. No wonder John Turner faltered. He didn't need at this point to call attention to the Prime Minister's speciousness. The Prime Minister had done that, far better than he could do. In fact the word *liar* did it. But he thought he must call attention to his own integrity, and he decided he could do so by confessing publicly to his part in the conspiracy of the Evil One against a former, real, Mulroney. He made this fatal confession to a select group of reporters, and asked that what he revealed must be accepted as information only, not quoted. The reporters almost hooted when they heard his submission. They kept their word not to quote him. In fact, they didn't believe him. Instead, they faithfully used the received information as the basis of the privileged though unsupported, unanimous opinion that John Turner was completely unfit to govern the nation as Prime Minister, believe you me. At this time, the election was only a few days, a few TV nights away. When it came, the country broke apart. It split three ways. Just under half the votes went for Mulroney. Just over half went against him. Winning with forty per cent of the votes a majority of the seats in the House, the Prime Minister's first task was to assure the divided electorate how democratic his mandate was: half of the people had spoken, the other half must obey. He had in fact elbowed his way into office like a man suspended from a hang-glider; even his elbows seemed unreal. When he invited the Canada he had unnecessarily wedged apart to unite and follow him confidently into the twenty-first century he seemed to be dancing an eighteenth-century minuet to music by a military band. Already puzzled by what to make of President Ronald Reagan's achievements, history will have some assistance with Mulroney's. He has already become an accessory to our living folklore. The legend of the Baie-Comeau angel has become a shining jewel of our cultural heritage. Need we despair of our identity, as long as the story, painted on nylon canvas and varnished with acrylic satire, of the Baie-Comeau angel's great love for our murdered leader, lives on in our hearts? That this legend owes its provenance to the Evil One, hardly matters. We have made it our own.

Acknowledgements

"The Lice" was first published in *Prism* 2.1 (Fall 1960): 34-57. The story was reprinted by Rudy Wiebe in his *Stories from Western Canada* (Toronto: Macmillan, 1972): 240-67, and again in *West of Fiction*, eds. Leah Flater, Aritha van Herk, and Rudy Wiebe (Edmonton: NeWest Press, 1983): 341-64. "The Lice" was also reprinted in *Not to be Taken at Night: Thirteen Classic Canadian Tales of Mystery and the Supernatural*, selected by John Robert Colombo and Michael Richardson (Toronto: Lester & Orpen Dennys, 1981): 108-36.

"Four Times Four Is Canada" was first published in *Alphabet* 7 (December 1963). It was republished in *Rainshadow: Stories from Vancouver Island*, eds. Ron Smith and Stephen Guppy (Lantzville: Oolichan Books; Victoria: Sono Nis Press, 1982): 211-35.

"Mettre en conte le dream" was first published in *Line* 14 (Fall 1989): 143-55.